A FLICKER IN THE NIGHT

Detectives hunt a serial killer who plays with fire

JOHN DEAN

THE
BOOK
FOLKS

Paperback published by The Book Folks

London, 2019

© John Dean

ISBN 978-1-6887-9335-4

www.thebookfolks.com

A Flicker in the Night is the seventh novel in a series of British murder mysteries featuring Detective Chief Inspector John Blizzard. Head to the back of this book for details of the author's other titles.

Chapter one

There are some faces that never fade from memory, some crimes so vile that they can never be forgiven, and some men whose names simply cannot be forgotten. Not now. Not ever. Reginald Morris is one such man. It is not that the northern city of Hafton has not tried to forget him. It's just that for many of its residents, out of sight is not out of mind. Every time dusk falls and the streetlights come on, people remember Reginald Morris. Darkness was his time, you see. Is still his time.

* * *

Sitting in his office that rainy afternoon, Detective Chief Inspector John Blizzard wished that he could say that he was immune from such thoughts, that he was a hard-headed policeman who regarded Reginald Morris as just another criminal safely locked away. However, Blizzard, like every officer involved in the inquiry, had been affected in some way. That is because even when he finally lies lifeless in his cold and neglected grave, Reginald Morris will live on.

Sitting and staring at the sheet of A4 paper lying on the desk, with its scrawled handwriting, Blizzard recalled the dark days that had cast such a long shadow over the city. Still cast a long shadow. Morris may be an elderly man now but, even though he has been locked up for two decades, the families of his victims are not free. Sure as night follows day, Reginald Morris comes back to haunt them as darkness falls. When they draw the curtains, switch off the television and head upstairs, they are reminded of their loved ones and every time they remember, Reginald Morris is with them and the tears come flooding back once again.

Thoughtfully reaching out to touch the piece of paper, Blizzard recalled how Morris came to him in his quieter moments: when he stood on the riverbank at dusk, turning up his collar against the chill breeze and staring over at the twinkling lights of the chemical plants on the south side of the water; when he was walking along a deserted night-time street with the rain glistening on the pavement and fish and chip papers scattered and windblown; when he lay in bed at night, shaken awake by dreams and thinking of the baby sleeping peacefully in the next room.

It was all tosh, of course, this worrying. Blizzard knew that Morris would never be released yet he still exerted a hold like no other criminal. Blizzard had locked up murderers, rapists, armed robbers, the lot, yet none had stayed with him the way that Reginald Morris had. The passage of the years could not dim the memory of the gleam in his eyes, soften the contours of his bony cheeks or disguise the cruel lines of his lips.

And why, this wet Friday afternoon, had a single sheet of paper prompted John Blizzard to think about the fire-starter? What had brought him to mind as the inspector sat quietly in the gathering gloom of his office at Abbey Road Police Station, listening to the raindrops pattering on the window and summoning the energy to stand up and switch on the light? Well, it was the poetry. One of Morris's trademarks was the disturbing verse which he sent to the police after each killing and which continued even after he had been arrested by a young CID officer called John Blizzard.

It was not particularly good poetry – there had been a uniform sergeant who had had his work published in some obscure anthology and he described Morris's efforts as doggerel – but the words seemed nevertheless to possess a power all of their own, even to an un-literary man such as Blizzard.

Feel her growing in the darkness deep inside,
Breathing, waiting, reaching out to the light,
Her strength slowly building away from human eye,
Pulsing strong within the furnace of the heart.

Soon she will burst forth and scorch a fiery swathe
Upon her blazing tail, one million howling devils,
Crying to the heavens, let loose a Hell on earth
And consume alive those who sleep at dead of night...

And so on, screeds of it. The latest piece, the first in twenty years, had arrived at Abbey Road that morning, in a plain brown envelope bearing a Hafton postmark and with Blizzard's name written in spidery handwriting on the front. It had been a particularly busy Friday for the detective, and it was only as the late afternoon darkness began to descend that Blizzard found it lying on his desk. Having read the verse, the initial instinct of most officers would have been to dismiss it as a crank, someone trying it on, but when it came to Reginald Morris, people tended to think much darker thoughts. It was his legacy to the city and, as he read it for the third time, Blizzard became more and more uneasy. Instinctively – despite himself – he glanced round to check he was alone in the office.

Angrily, he rebuked himself for his nervousness, placed the poem carefully in his desk drawer and stared pensively out of the window for several minutes, cradling a mug of tea which had long grown cold. Then he slowly picked up the desk telephone and dialled the number of the mental hospital fifteen miles from Hafton where Reginald Morris had been held since his conviction for his arson attacks.

'I'm sorry to trouble you,' he said, 'but this is Detective Chief Inspector John Blizzard at Hafton Police. Can you put me through to Hazel Myers?'

A few moments later, a woman came on the line.

'Inspector,' she said. 'Long time no speak. What can I do for you?'

'I know it's an odd question, Hazel, but Reginald Morris is still a patient with you, isn't he?'

'It is an odd question, Chief Inspector. Surely you, of all people, should know that he is not going anywhere.'

'Yeah, of course,' replied Blizzard. 'Thank you.'

'Any reason why you ask?'

'No, nothing really.' Blizzard glanced at the poetry. 'Sorry to have wasted your time.'

Replacing the receiver, he shook his head.

'Maybe the Super's right,' he said. 'Maybe I do need a holiday. Take Fee and the little one away somewhere.'

The rain drove harder against the window.

'Somewhere sunny and warm,' he said. 'Forget all this nonsense.'

However, he did not throw the piece of paper away, opting instead to leave it in the drawer before walking briskly from the office. The mysterious verse remained in the drawer until the early hours of Monday, when an old man called Albert Pembridge breathed his last.

Chapter two

It was ironic, thought Blizzard as he stood outside the terraced house with the smell of smoke hanging thick in the night air, and the darkness illuminated by flashing blue lights, that Albert Pembridge was probably creating much more concern in death than he ever had when he was alive. That was because the demise of just another anonymous old man had assumed great importance to the detective and he was struggling to rationalise his thoughts as he entered the building and climbed the stairs to the first second floor flat.

Pembridge was already dead when Blue Watch arrived at 72 Inkerman Street shortly after three thirty. The top floor flat of the three-storey Victorian house was well alight and a crowd of people, many in dressing gowns, had gathered to watch in silence, a flickering half-light dancing across their upturned faces as flames shot into the night air through windows shattered by the intense heat. Having confirmed that the residents of the other flats were accounted for, the firefighters had donned breathing apparatus and battled their way up the narrow stairs, smashing their way into the flat and shrinking back as the rush of air gave the fire new life. It was a last roar of defiance, though, and it was all over within a few minutes as the torrent of water doused the flames.

Blizzard had arrived half an hour later, unshaven, brown hair tousled and uncombed, tie dangling loosely round his neck and jacket collar half turned up, the garments thrown on when the call from the control room jerked him from dreams in which Reginald Morris kept appearing. Reginald Morris was like that. You ask anyone who ever met him. Now Blizzard stood at the door to the flat, eyes glowing white in the gloom, nose wrinkled as the acrid smell of smoke caught the back of his throat.

'Where's the Watch Commander?' he asked.

'In the kitchen,' said one of the firefighters. 'If you say pretty please, he might make you a cup of tea.'

Blizzard allowed himself a faint smile, well used to the black humour of firefighters, and picked his way across the crunching cinders before entering the kitchen where Tom Spivey was crouched down, peering into the oven.

'I'm hoping you'll say it's a gas blast, Tom,' said Blizzard. 'Save me a lot of work. A discarded fag will do.'

''Fraid not, John,' said Spivey, straightening up. 'This one's got dodgy written all over it.'

'Where's chummy?'

'On the bed.' Spivey rubbed a hand across his grimy brow. 'Be warned, he's not a pretty sight.'

'They never are.'

Blizzard walked into the bedroom, shone his torch onto the old man's charred body and gasped as the beam illuminated the blistered face, leering through crooked yellow teeth. Pembridge's frail body had been consumed by a fire which had left his bony limbs twisted, his wrinkled skin peeling and his mouth distorted as the smoke filled his bursting lungs and strangled the scream in his throat.

'I've seen some things,' said Spivey, with a shake of the head as he looked over the detective's shoulder, 'but never that bad. Have you?'

'Once,' said Blizzard. 'A long time ago. I take it you are sure that it's arson?'

'Have to see what our investigators say but it certainly spread very quickly. Trouble is, there's so much muck and grease in these places that fire can do that sometimes – and there's no smoke alarm. We don't know how long it smouldered beforehand either. Maybe the old fellow did fall asleep in bed with a fag in his hand. Wouldn't be the first time.'

'But it could be arson?'

'If it was, it would mean someone poured an accelerant over the old guy. I mean, you'd have to be a sicko to do that. Someone like...'

'Yes, thank you,' said Blizzard.

'Best not to think it, eh? Anyway, we're finished here. It's all yours now.'

'Thanks a bunch.'

Blizzard watched the firefighters pack up and listened to the clank of equipment, the tramp of heavy boots and the banter as they clumped downstairs and onto the street. For a second, he was lost in thoughts of events more than twenty years previously. Then, with an effort, he dragged himself back to the present day.

'I'm just being stupid,' he said. 'Daft old bastard probably fell asleep with a tab in his mouth, like Tom says.'

Blizzard lashed his torch round the room one last time, the beam coming to rest again on the corpse's grinning face.

'Don't know what you're laughing at, Albert, old son,' muttered the detective. He set off down the stairs to find the uniformed inspector to discuss securing the flat until daylight. 'Your problems are over, I've got them now.'

Chapter three

It was a typically dull northern winter morning as, after only a few hours' snatched sleep, a thick-headed John Blizzard kissed goodbye to Fee and baby Michael, left his home in a small village to the west of Hafton and drove through the leafy fringes of the city towards Abbey Road Police Station. A gentle drizzle fell from the leaden skies and he cursed: Blizzard hated Mondays. He cursed, too, when a few moments later a school bus lurched out of a side road, forcing him to brake sharply. The inspector flashed his headlights angrily at the driver but all he received in return was two fingers stuck out of the window.

'No fucking respect,' growled Blizzard.

Moments later, journey complete and still muttering about bus drivers, he turned into a tree-lined lane at the end of which stood a labyrinth of single-storey interlocking cabins. This was Abbey Road Police Station, opened supposedly as a temporary measure and still here more than 30 years later, the green paint peeling, the windows grimy and the roof leaking.

Blizzard, who had always worked in Hafton, virtually all of it plainclothes, and had been promoted to take charge of the Western division CID several years previously, was usually too busy to worry about the state of the police station. He parked his car and headed for the office of Detective Superintendent Arthur Ronald, his direct superior. A few minutes later, Ronald, a pudgy, balding man with ruddy cheeks, sat watching his old friend as Blizzard slumped in his seat, eyes closed and cradling a mug of steaming tea in his hand.

'You look shit,' said Ronald.

'Thank you for those kind words. Didn't get much sleep.'

'And this time you can't blame the nipper. Tell me about this fire.'

'The dead man is one Albert Pembridge.' Blizzard opened his eyes and took a sip of tea. 'An old drunk fallen on hard times.'

'I gather the fire brigade is not very happy about it.'

'I don't suppose Albert Pembridge is turning cartwheels but, for what it's worth, it looks dodgy, yes. That's what Tom Spivey thinks, anyway.'

There was silence for a few moments as Ronald considered how to broach the next subject. The two men went back a long way but they were still very different. Ronald, a smart dresser with a sharply pressed suit, tie always done up and shoes shined, was a charming man with an easy manner but one who was always careful what he said. Blizzard was different: said what he thought and rarely considered the consequences. And this time, Arthur Ronald could see plenty of consequences.

'Any truth in the rumour that it's one of Les Melcham's places?' he asked. He tried to make the comment sound casual. As if it didn't matter.

'Might be.'

'Well if it is, I expect you to carry out the inquiry with painstaking professionalism. We've had enough trouble with him and his lawyer.' Ronald fixed Blizzard with a steely glare. 'Understand?'

'You know me.' Blizzard drained the last of his tea, stood up and headed for the door.

'That's why I said it. I mean, you're hardly on each other's Christmas card lists, are you?'

'No, but...'

'I mean it, John.'

Blizzard stood at the door for a moment, noted the superintendent's stern expression and nodded.

'I'll behave,' he said.

'You see that you do.'

Blizzard was still thinking about Les Melcham as he drove through the busy morning traffic and turned off the congested main road into Inkerman Street, a place he already knew well. Only three months previously, he and Detective Sergeant David Colley had investigated the murder of a drug pusher by an addict out of his head on heroin in one of the street's squalid flats. One of Les Melcham's flats. Melcham had not liked the police attention then and he would not like it now.

Melcham, in the inspector's view, was a leech who symbolised Inkerman Street's fall from grace and many streets like it. Once home to respectable families, it had fallen on hard times as gradually its houses were bought up by hawkish landlords such as Melcham. Out for a quick profit, he and his ilk had converted the houses into flats populated with a tawdry mix of drug addicts, drop-outs, prostitutes and alcoholics.

As Blizzard drove into Inkerman Street, he thought about Albert Pembridge, whose life had fallen apart when he was made redundant by a local engineering firm. For Albert Pembridge, life was never the same again. He held a number of poorly paid jobs, all of which he lost as he started drinking and became increasingly unreliable. As his drinking grew worse, his wife left him, his family wanted nothing to do with him and he ended up living in an alcoholic haze in the flat in Inkerman Street.

Blizzard knew all this thanks to a phone call from Colley and, as he pulled up outside the house, he saw the sergeant waiting for him. A tall, lean man, at five foot eleven a couple of inches taller than Blizzard, with close-cropped dark hair, honest eyes, pronounced cheekbones and a mouth which always seemed about to curl into a smile, Colley was smartly dressed in black trousers and grey jacket.

Blizzard got out of the car and strode across the street, his feet crunching on broken glass from the top floor windows.

'Come up with anything else?' he asked.

'Just confirmation of what I said on the phone,' said Colley. 'The old fellow was rarely sober.'

'What about his family?'

'His wife lives in Australia, apparently, went to live there with some bloke she met in a pub. He hasn't got any kids. And, as far as I see, he did not really have any friends. Most of what I've been able to pick up is neighbour tittle-tattle.'

'Anyone know if he smoked?'

'Like a chimney.' Colley led the way into the house. 'I said we'd meet our forensics guy in the flat. There's a fire brigade investigator up there as well.'

Stepping into the flat, the smell of stale smoke hit them immediately. By daylight, the full extent of the fire became clear and they stood in silence and surveyed the blackened walls, the scorched carpet and the charred furniture. A quick glance around the room at what remained of the rickety armchair and the outdated television set balancing precariously on a wonky table, confirmed that Albert Pembridge lived in poverty. The detectives stepped over the empty cheap wine bottles littering the floor and entered the bedroom, where they found the fire brigade investigator.

'Elaine Harrison,' she said, extending a hand.

'John Blizzard. Any ideas?'

'My money's on arson,' she said. 'Probably some kind of accelerant. Wouldn't take much to set this lot alight. A lot of the furniture is very old and would burn extremely easily.'

'No sign of a break-in,' said the forensics officer, appearing from the kitchen.

'What about evidence of a struggle?' asked Blizzard.

'Difficult to say. Nothing obvious.'

'It just doesn't add up.' Blizzard shook his head. 'If it was an opportunistic crime – a thief starting the fire to cover his tracks – the perpetrator is unlikely to have climbed two flights of stairs in the pitch black, is he? He'd have gone for the downstairs flat, wouldn't he?'

'You'd think,' said Colley. He gestured to the table. 'And what did Pembridge have worth stealing, anyway? We're not exactly talking Antiques Roadshow, are we?'

The sergeant noticed the expression on Blizzard's face.

'I got into it when Laura had that bug a few weeks ago,' he said. 'They repeat it in the middle of the night. Very stimulating.'

Blizzard gave a nod of understanding; he'd been there with the baby.

'Besides,' continued Colley. 'I quite like a spot of Fiona Bruce at two in the morning.'

'Yes, thank you, Sergeant. I don't need to know about the sordid workings of your mind. Can we concentrate on the job at hand, do you think?'

'Sorry,' said the sergeant. 'If we rule out an opportunistic crime, that means that someone deliberately killed Albert Pembridge – and why would anyone want to kill an old drunk?'

'Indeed. No friends I get, but enemies?' Blizzard headed for the door. 'Come on, let's ask a few more questions of the good burghers of Inkerman Street and see if they can tell us.'

Once out in the street, Blizzard watched as a middle-aged woman in a headscarf detached herself from the little knot of people who had gathered to survey the scene.

'This is Glenda Pressley,' said Colley as the woman approached them. 'She has given us a lot of the information about Albert Pembridge.'

'And you were a friend, were you?' asked Blizzard.

'Not really,' said Glenda. 'You just pick things up. I don't think Albert had any friends.'

'Perhaps if he had, this might not have happened,' said Blizzard and walked towards his car.

Glenda looked at the sergeant.

'He's very rude, isn't he?'

'He is,' said the sergeant. He set off after his boss. 'But he's usually right.'

As Blizzard unlocked his car, his mobile phone rang. He took the call.

'It's Control,' said a woman's disembodied voice. 'Can you attend the General Hospital for the post-mortem on Albert Pembridge? Ask for Mr Reynolds.'

'Will do.' Blizzard slipped the phone back into his pocket and turned to the sergeant. 'Our cup overfloweth, the Angel of Death wants to see us.'

Chapter four

Half an hour later, the detectives were standing in the sanitised atmosphere of the hospital post-mortem room, watching Home Office pathologist Peter Reynolds as he dissected the scorched remains of Albert Pembridge with what could only be described as gusto. Reynolds, a balding middle-aged little man with piggy eyes twinkling out of a chubby face, smiled as he noticed the policemen wrinkle their noses to block out the pungent smell. Long experience had taught him that it wasn't the blood and gore that turned police officers' stomachs but the sickly aroma. Personally, he'd grown used to it years ago and in a perverse way rather liked it, even joking that it made it easier to bear the smell of his wife's cooking, a joke that never failed to offend at dinner parties to his eternal delight.

Now, he straightened up and rinsed his hands in a sink.

'Well?' asked Blizzard impatiently.

'No, he's not,' said Reynolds in his slightly nasal voice.

'He went through seven years of medical school to be able to deduce that,' said Blizzard. He glanced at the sergeant. 'Money well spent, eh?'

Colley grinned. He was going to enjoy himself; everyone knew that Reynolds and Blizzard detested each other and the sergeant always found himself in demand from colleagues keen to hear every detail of their encounters.

'Investigation not going well, Chief Inspector?' asked Reynolds.

'No, it isn't. Mainly because I don't know what I'm supposed to be investigating. Are you going to help me make my mind up?'

'I'll need to do some more work, but I'd say that your man burned to death.'

'I could have worked that out for myself.'

'Not necessarily.' Reynolds reached for a towel and wiped his hands. 'As I am sure you know, most fire victims die from smoke inhalation but the evidence here points to him being alive when the burns were inflicted. And the degenerative nature of his illness meant he was unable to save himself.'

'What illness?' asked Blizzard.

'You didn't know?'

'I knew he wasn't going to compete in the next Olympics.'

'Somewhat of an understatement, Chief Inspector. Albert Pembridge was a very sick man indeed. He had well-advanced lung cancer, presumably brought on by heavy smoking over many years.'

'How sick was he?' asked Colley. He looked at the twisted remains of the old man. 'There wasn't much on him.'

'I'd have given him six months. Maybe a little more.'

'Could he have committed suicide?'

'The man was a chronic alcoholic,' said the pathologist. 'My guess is that he was so drunk last night that such deliberate thought would have been beyond him. No, I can only see two alternatives: that he fell asleep and dropped his cigarette, or someone set him on fire. And my money's on the latter option.'

'I was afraid you might say that,' said Blizzard.

'You had better hope that I am wrong,' said the pathologist. 'Because the last time I saw something this sick, it was…'

'Yes, thank you.' Blizzard headed for the door. 'This isn't time for irresponsible speculation.'

'But isn't Inkerman Street in the same area where—'

'Yes, it is.' Blizzard opened the door. 'But I hardly think that's relevant, do you? Good day to you, Mr Reynolds.'

The pathologist watched the detectives go. Then, with a shake of the head, he returned back to his work.

* * *

'It's all people are talking about,' said Colley as the detectives walked across the car park outside the hospital, turning their jacket collars up against the drizzle.

'I know it is, David, but he's been locked up for twenty years.'

'Yes, but it could be a copycat. Perhaps someone who read about it in the papers when they covered the twentieth anniversary a few weeks back.'

'Possibly,' said Blizzard. He unlocked the car. 'I just hope that forensics come up with a cigarette butt at the flat, that's all. I don't fancy being around when the media click. It was bad enough when Reginald Morris was at large.'

The officers drove slowly back to Inkerman Street, the chief inspector deep in thought, the sergeant maintaining a diplomatic silence. He knew better than to pursue the conversation.

When they walked into the old man's flat, head of forensics Detective Inspector Graham Ross, a handsome well-groomed fresh-faced young man with immaculate wavy brown hair and wearing his customary smart light grey suit and shiny shoes, was waiting for them.

'This is all a bit grubby for you, isn't it, Versace?' said Blizzard. 'If you're not careful you'll mucky your designer shoes.'

'No such worries for you, I would imagine,' replied Ross affably. He glanced at the chief inspector's scuffed brogues.

'So, what have you got for us?'

'You have been lucky.'

'So why don't I feel it?' Blizzard watched as Ross held up a transparent sachet containing a small blackened object. 'And what exactly is that supposed to be?'

'It's a spent match. God knows how it survived but it's a good sign that this is arson.'

'It's not enough on its own, though, is it? The old feller could have used it to light a fag.'

'Actually, I don't think he did,' said Colley. 'Pembridge only ever used a lighter. That's what Glenda Pressley told me. She gave it to him as a Christmas present after he almost set himself on fire when he dropped a lighted match into his lap. She said he never used anything else after that.'

Blizzard held the sachet up to the light.

'Gentlemen,' he said quietly, 'unless I am very much mistaken, this just became a murder investigation.'

Chapter five

Blizzard moved quickly following the discovery. By lunchtime, an incident room had been established at Abbey Road and Ronald had assigned him a large team of detectives and uniformed officers. The decision counted for little, however, as door-to-door questioning produced a paucity of fresh information about the dead man. So it was that shortly after seven thirty that evening, a gloomy Blizzard sat in his office, staring absently through the window into the night, his feet on the desk. His mood was equally dark; the inspector knew only too well that murder investigations which failed to produce an arrest within 24 hours usually became long drawn-out affairs. And always there was that nagging feeling about the poem still lying in his desk drawer.

His reverie was disturbed by a knock on the door, and Colley walked into the room.

'I was wondering if you fancied a swift one down The Abbey?' said Colley. 'It's Brian's birthday and I'm not sure there's much more we can do tonight.'

'What about Jan and the little 'un?'

'Away at the grandparents. So how about it?'

'No, I'd better get back.' Blizzard lowered his feet to the floor. 'Fee's had the baby all day. She'll be going up the wall. Listen, we're not missing anything, are we?'

'Good drinking time.' Colley turned towards the door. 'Something I intend to correct now.'

'Before you go, let's run through what we know about the old guy.'

'We know he was a loser.' Colley slumped into a seat. 'And that he smoked and drank heavily. Neighbours said that he'd buy cheap wine from the off-licence and by lunchtime he'd be rolling drunk. If he was really flush, he'd go to one of the local pubs and drink alone until they kicked him out.'

'So where did he get his money?'

'Benefits. Spent it all on booze and tabs. Hardly ever ate, was way behind on the gas and leccy, and social security paid his rent.'

'Didn't anyone try to help the poor sod?' asked Blizzard.

'Social services said he refused to let them in when they sent someone round a couple of months ago. The woman I talked to said he was very abusive; to be honest, she didn't sound that bothered. There's a thousand more where he came from.'

'So, if no one cared about an old soak like Albert Pembridge, who on earth would want to kill him?'

'Search me.'

'Did the ex-wife have any ideas?' asked Blizzard.

'Not really. Sarah tracked her down in Oz, but she hasn't been back since leaving and she wasn't in contact with him. Sarah got the impression that she wanted to forget him. She's not even coming over for the funeral. A distant relative in Cornwall is sorting out the arrangements but she last saw him fifteen years ago. It's almost as if people tried to wipe Albert Pembridge from their lives.'

'Well, now someone has done it for them,' said Blizzard. 'What about friends?'

'Didn't have any to speak of.'

'It just doesn't make sense.' Blizzard reached into his top drawer and handed over the poem. 'Read this and tell me what you think.'

Colley scanned the lines.

'Just another crank,' he said.

'That's what I thought until Pembridge died. The phraseology in the poem reminds me of Reginald Morris.'

'Copycat?'

'Could be. Morris is still inside. I checked with Crake Lane.'

'Why on earth do a thing like that? You said it yourself, Reginald Morris has got nothing to do with this.' He stood up. 'Come on, I'll buy you that pint.'

'Just the one,' said Blizzard. He put the poem carefully back into his top drawer, hauled his jacket from the back of his chair and followed his sergeant from the room. 'And you're right, this has nothing to do with Reginald Morris. I was silly to even think it.'

But Colley couldn't help feeling, as they walked down the corridor, that his boss didn't sound convinced.

* * *

The city centre clock had just intoned one in the morning when the man carrying the jerry can arrived in a deserted Holbrook Street. Glancing round to make sure that he had not been observed and keeping to the shadows, he approached number 57. The man stood outside the terraced house for a few moments, surveying the light filtering through the threadbare curtains drawn across the downstairs window. Edging closer, he could hear voices coming from inside the room and he stood and considered his next actions for a few moments.

The sound of footsteps further down the street had him shrinking into the shadows again. Looking closer, he could see that it was a young couple, arm in arm, clearly drunk. They entered one of the other houses and, after hearing the slam of the front door, the man returned his attention to number 57. Mind made up, it did not take him long to prise open the window and climb into the old man's ground floor flat. Although the light was on, Bill Lowther was asleep on the sofa where he had slumped in his drunken haze, his mouth open, snores guttural and his breath infused with the smell of alcohol. The television was still on – an old episode of *Midsomer Murders* – and the intruder gave a crooked smile. He had always appreciated irony.

Then he unscrewed the jerry can lid. By the time the first flames had started to consume Bill Lowther's body, and his would-be rescuers were hollering their frantic warnings and hammering on the door with their fists, the intruder had slipped through the window again and vanished back into the shadows.

Chapter six

That night, Blizzard had his first nightmare for months. It began as a flicker, deep within a city that was sleeping still and silent under a sky which had begun to glow a faint orange. Within seconds, tendrils of fire snaked through streets that were now thronged with terrified people, tearing at their burning clothes as they staggered from blazing houses, skin scorching and peeling, hair aflame, the night air rent with their screams and echoing with the shrill of distant sirens which never seemed to get any closer.

It took the confused and sweat-soaked chief inspector some moments to realise that he had jerked awake and the sirens were the insistent ringing of his mobile phone on the bedside table. Snapping on the light, the inspector glanced blearily at his watch and groaned.

'Who the hell's that?' grumbled Fee, lying next to him. She cursed as the baby started crying in the next room. 'Whoever it is, I'll bloody well kill them.'

Blizzard picked up the phone. It was Colley.

'This had better be good,' said the inspector into the device as he watched Fee pad across the room without opening her eyes. 'In case you hadn't noticed, it's two thirty in the sodding morning.'

'Yeah, sorry about that,' said Colley.

'Still, you've probably done me a favour. I was having an awful nightmare about people burning to death.'

'I'm afraid it just came true. We've had another bad fire. Holbrook Street. Round the corner from Inkerman Street.'

Suddenly wide awake, Blizzard sat up, head clearing, senses sharp.

'And that's not the only coincidence,' continued the sergeant. 'I think you'd better get over here ASAP.'

'On my way.'

Blizzard ended the call, acutely aware that his heart was pounding and that his throat was dry.

'What the hell is happening here?' he murmured.

The inspector dressed hurriedly and walked out onto the landing to see Fee emerge from the bedroom with the baby in her arms.

'Where are you going?' she asked.

'Sorry, love. Duty calls. You know how it is.'

She nodded. Fee, a police officer's daughter who was on maternity leave from her job as a detective constable, had experienced this many times. As ever, when Blizzard was called out in the early hours, childhood memories of watching her father disappear into the night stirred and, a couple of minutes later, she stood at the living room window, cradling the now sleeping baby, and watched in silence as the inspector backed the car down the drive. When the vehicle had disappeared, Fee Ellis sighed and turned back into the room.

* * *

All manner of thoughts ranged through the inspector's mind as he negotiated the winding country roads to emerge onto deserted city streets, eventually entering the grubby world of bedsit land, passing Albert Pembridge's flat before turning into Holbrook Street and pulling up behind the fire engines. The stench of smoke still hung heavy in the crisp night air as Blizzard got out of the car and joined his sergeant to gaze in grim silence at the flashing blue lights and the crowd of people watching as the firefighters of Blue Watch packed up their gear.

'I think I preferred the nightmare,' said Blizzard. 'What do we know?'

'Neighbours reckon it's a chap called Lowther, a seventy-two-year-old widower. Came home to his flat sometime after midnight, seems to have fallen asleep on the sofa and next thing anyone knows, the place is on fire. A couple of young lads from other flats tried to get in but were beaten back by the flames. Couple of heroes, by the sound of it. One of them has gone to hospital for treatment to burns on his hands.'

'Where had the old guy been?'

'The local club – he goes down to meet old workmates and sink a few pints and play dominoes on a Monday night. They used to work in the shipyards together.'

'Any word on the cause of the fire?'

'The window was open so, if it does turn out to be iffy, that could be where the arsonists got in. Spivey can tell you more than me.'

Colley gestured to the firefighter pushing his way through the throng of neighbours in front of the house. Spivey walked over to them, removed his helmet and wearily ran a hand through his sweat-streaked hair.

'This is becoming a habit, gentlemen,' he said.

'Same as last night?' asked Blizzard.

'I am afraid so. Very fierce, spread quickly, body badly burned. Oh, and this house didn't have smoke alarms. Just like Inkerman Street.' He gave them an exasperated look. 'We keep telling the landlords to fit them but some of them ignore the advice.'

'Which is where the coincidence comes in,' said Colley. 'This is another of Les Melcham's houses.'

'Now, isn't that an interesting little link?' said Blizzard, with a gleam in his eye. 'Definitely time to have a chat with our Les, I think.'

'The Super won't like it.'

'Nevertheless.' The inspector pushed open the front gate. 'Come on, let's take a look inside.'

'One of the lads who tried to rescue the old fella is still in there,' said Colley. 'Young chap called Andy Hemmings. You might want to start with him.'

The detectives had to cover their faces with handkerchiefs as they walked along the smoky hallway and climbed the stairs to the first-floor landing where Colley knocked on a door. It was opened tentatively by a pale young man in his late teens, unshaven with tousled fair hair and dressed in a jumper and jeans hurriedly thrown over pyjamas. On seeing their warrant cards, Andy Hemmings nodded, ushered them into his cramped little flat and gestured to a dilapidated sofa, which sagged alarmingly as the policemen sat down.

'We'd like to ask you a few questions if you feel up to it,' said Blizzard.

'I'll try,' said the young man. He sat down on a threadbare armchair. 'But I feel a bit shaky.'

'That's understandable,' said Blizzard. 'The sergeant here says that you showed great courage in trying to rescue Mr Lowther. Where were you when the fire started?'

'I'd gone to bed early. I've been overdoing the studying. I'm an English Literature student at the university. I was woken by someone yelling that there was a fire so I ran downstairs.'

'What did you see?' asked Blizzard.

'Not much, it's a dim light in the hall and there was smoke everywhere, but I could hear Bill screaming...' Hemmings paused for a moment, fighting back the tears. 'Edward was already there.'

'Edward?' Blizzard looked at Colley. 'Who's he?'

'The other lad I mentioned. Edward Jones. He has the other ground floor flat – opposite Bill. He tried to get in but was beaten back by the flames. He's gone to hospital.'

Andrew looked at the policemen anxiously.

'Is he alright?' he asked.

'It's not too serious,' said Colley. 'What happened then, Andrew?'

'I tried to get into Bill's flat but it was just too hot...' The student lapsed into silence for a few moments. 'There were flames everywhere. It was truly awful.'

'You did all you could,' said Blizzard. 'How well did you know Bill Lowther?'

'Just to nod to.'

'He'd been out, I think? Could he have been drunk when he got back?'

'It wouldn't surprise me,' said Hemmings. 'He liked his beer, did Bill. Especially on a Monday night with his pals.'

'Had there been any trouble here over the past few days?' asked Blizzard.

'Trouble?' The student looked startled by the question. 'Surely you don't think it's deliberate.'

'It's a possibility. It's very like the fire over at Inkerman Street last night and we think that was started deliberately.'

'Why would anyone want to kill an old bloke like Bill?' asked Hemmings.

'If I knew that,' said Blizzard, standing up, 'we wouldn't be having this conversation. Thank you for your time, Andy. One of my officers will take a fuller statement from you in the morning when you're feeling a bit better.'

'I'm afraid I haven't been very helpful,' said Hemmings as he opened the door to the flat to let them out.

'You tried to save him, that's a lot more than most of the people round here would have done,' replied Blizzard. 'Good night, Andy.'

As the detectives walked down the stairs and into the hall, they were confronted by Acting Uniform Inspector

Charlie Johnson ushering another young man through the front door. Blizzard glanced at the bandaged hands.

'I take it you are Edward Jones,' he said. 'Are you alright to talk?'

'Yeah, I think so.' Jones glanced at the firefighters crowded round the door to Bill Lowther's flat and shook his head. 'I can't believe this has happened.'

Blizzard studied him for a few moments, trying to get the measure of the young man. Edward Jones was a touch older than Andy Hemmings, also unshaven, with lank short dark hair and a thin face streaked by grime. His white T-shirt and jeans were stained black. He was clearly badly shaken by his ordeal.

'What do you want to know?' asked Jones as he let them into his untidy ground floor flat and slumped heavily into an armchair.

Blizzard took in the squalid surroundings and shook his head. As a new father, the thought that his son could one day end up living in a place like this disturbed the detective. In that moment, Blizzard's distaste for Les Melcham and his ilk burned bright. He walked over to the window and stared out through the tattered curtains at the flashing blue lights in the street. Colley noted his boss's reverie, sat down on the ramshackle sofa, and began the questioning.

'Were you awake when the fire started?' he asked.

'Yeah. I'd not been back long. I'd been out with some of the lads from work.'

'Which is where?'

'I'm an electrician for Hodgsons on the Belle Vue Trading Estate. It was one of the lads' birthday.'

'We know them well,' said Blizzard. He turned back from his perusal of the street. 'We nicked the manager for deception a few months back.'

'I heard.' Jones closed his eyes. 'Look, I'm a bit shaken up, can you get your questions over with, please?'

'Of course,' said Colley with an understanding nod of the head. 'So, you'd been out to the pub.'

'Yeah, I had just decided to turn in when I heard Bill screaming.'

'I take it that was the first you knew that something was wrong,' said Blizzard. 'There aren't any smoke alarms here, I believe.'

'Yeah, that's right. And the wiring's crap. We keep telling the landlord but he doesn't take any notice. I offered to fix it myself but he told me not to.'

'Typical of Les Melcham,' said Blizzard.

'You know him?'

'I know him. Were you the first one into the hall?'

'I think so, but it was all a bit chaotic and I couldn't see much, what with the smoke. I tried to get into Bill's flat and next thing I knew someone was helping me into an ambulance.' Jones looked anxious. 'Is Andy alright?'

'He's OK,' said Blizzard. 'You've both been very brave. Did Bill ever have any trouble with anyone?'

'Na, Bill was a nice old bloke...' Jones shot the chief inspector the same appalled look the detective had seen on Hemmings' face. 'Surely you don't believe ...?'

'I don't know what to believe.' Blizzard stood up. 'Thank you for your time anyway. We'll talk to you again in the morning.'

Jones shot the inspector an anxious look.

'You won't tell Les Melcham that I said anything about the wiring, will you?' he said.

'Les give you trouble, does he?'

'I'm saying nothing.'

'You're alright, we won't mention your name,' said Blizzard. He eyed the damp patches on the peeling wallpaper and let his gaze roam down the wall to the electrical socket hanging off the wall. 'We know what Les Melcham's like.'

With a thin smile, Blizzard led the way across the hall and into Bill Lowther's flat, nodding a greeting to the firefighters as he did so. The orange glow filtering into the living room from the streetlights confirmed that, like Albert Pembridge's home, the flat had been destroyed: walls blackened, carpet thick with soot, furnishings charred, and the air heavily laden with smoke. The badly burned body of Bill Lowther was slumped on the sofa, and it was clear from the agonised expression on the face that he had also died a truly horrible death.

'This was no electrical fault,' said Blizzard.

'No way,' said Colley.

Charlie Johnson walked up behind the detectives.

'Whoever is doing this is a sicko,' he said quietly. 'It reminds me of R...'

'Yes. Well, it isn't,' snapped Blizzard. He stalked out of the house into the chill night air.

'Was it something I said?' asked the inspector as he and Colley walked out after him.

'Reginald Morris is a touchy subject right now,' said Colley.

'I'm not surprised. Wait till the newspapers put two and two together and start to dredge it all up again. They'll have the old bastard's face plastered all over the front pages.'

'That's what he's afraid of,' said Colley. 'He loves publicity, does Reggie Morris.'

The sergeant walked over to join the chief inspector who was standing, shoulders hunched, hands thrust into pockets, staring morosely back at the house. Fire investigator Elaine Harrison walked over.

'Arson?' asked the inspector.

'I need to do a more thorough investigation of the scene, but I'd say that it's the same as last night.'

Blizzard looked at Colley.

'I think we'll pull our friend Mr Melcham in later today,' said the inspector. 'There are some questions I'd like answered.'

'Too true,' said the sergeant.

Chapter seven

Detective Superintendent Arthur Ronald called a press conference shortly before 10am. Adding to the sombre mood at Abbey Road Police Station was a tip-off from the press office that the event would be dominated by the name Reginald Morris. Not surprisingly, the tension was almost tangible to David Colley as he leant against a wall, watching the media circus with interest while the briefing room buzzed with the excited whispers of the reporters. The journalists went quiet when the two senior detectives entered to take their places at the front, cameras clicking as the newspaper photographers captured the striking image of the two stern officers leading the hunt for a potential serial killer.

'Thank you for your attendance, ladies and gentlemen,' said Ronald gravely. 'As you know, this city has seen two fatal arson attacks inside twenty-four hours. The press office has ensured that you have the relevant information, and myself and Detective Chief Inspector Blizzard are happy to answer any of your questions.'

Colley allowed himself a faint smile. Happy was not the word he would have used to describe John Blizzard when he heard that Reginald Morris would be mentioned.

Blizzard's dislike of the media was legendary, and the focus on Morris had darkened his mood even further.

However, the first question was innocuous enough.

'Do you believe these are random killings?' asked one of the reporters. 'Or is there a pattern? Are you looking for a serial killer?'

'There are certain similarities,' replied Ronald. He was choosing his words carefully. 'That would lead us to think it possible that the same person was responsible.'

A murmur ran round the room.

'Can you elaborate on that?' asked another voice.

'Both victims were retired men, lived alone in the same area and had consumed significant quantities of alcohol before their deaths. However, our investigations have been unable to find any reason why they should be targeted.'

'Do you have any comment to make on the nature of these men's deaths?' asked another reporter.

'They were particularly senseless crimes without any conceivable motive,' said Ronald. Long experience told him that the question was designed to elicit a juicy quote for the reporters' copy. 'Whoever is doing this is a sick individual preying on the most vulnerable people in our society.'

The reporters scribbled furiously and Colley smiled slightly; it was always a pleasure to watch Arthur Ronald handle the media. Blizzard, for his part, was content to leave it to his boss.

'Do you think he may strike again?' asked another journalist.

'I think that is entirely possible.'

'Do you have any suspects yet?'

'No.'

'Do you have any advice for the people living in the area?' asked a radio reporter.

'They must be extremely vigilant until we apprehend this individual,' replied the superintendent. The routine nature of the questioning was causing him to hope that the tip-off about Reginald Morris had been wrong.

But it was not, and the next question froze the smile on his face as a sharply-dressed young man stood up.

'Gary Mistry, The Daily Herald,' he said.

'Yes, Gary.' Ronald tried not to look concerned.

'Am I right in thinking that the last time Hafton experienced something like this, several of the fires were in the Inkerman Street area?'

'That is correct,' said Ronald. 'However, I do not—'

'And that for both this city and the two of you in particular, the last two nights have evoked bad memories?'

'I do not know what you mean,' replied Ronald blandly, trying to buy time.

'Then let me make it clear,' said the journalist. 'I refer to the case of Reginald Morris. I understand that as young officers both of you worked on the inquiry and, DCI Blizzard, I believe that you were the one who arrested him.'

'His case has no bearing on this investigation,' said Blizzard. It was the first time he had spoken since sitting down, and the reporters leaned forward, pens poised above notepads. 'Reginald Morris has been locked away for the past twenty years. He is history.'

'But are there not uncanny similarities? Could you not be dealing with a copycat?'

'I do not believe that to be the case.'

'But how can you be sure, Chief Inspector?' asked Mistry. 'It took your force a long time to catch Reginald Morris due to a series of failings in the investigation. What if history is about to repeat itself?'

'I am afraid that is all the questions I intend to answer,' said Blizzard. He stood up abruptly. 'Good day, ladies and gentlemen, I have a murder investigation to run.'

And with a face like thunder, he stalked from the room, followed by an embarrassed Ronald and a frowning Colley.

Out in the corridor, Blizzard cursed and banged a fist against the wall.

'How dare he?' he exclaimed angrily.

'He was only doing his job,' said Ronald.

'The last thing we want is the papers dragging up a twenty-year-old case, though!' Blizzard started walking down the corridor. 'Mistry was well out of order.'

'You were the one who was out of order,' said Ronald, catching him up. His attempt to keep control of his temper had failed within seconds. 'What do you think you are playing at – walking out like that? That's only going to make things worse. You know what Mistry is like.'

'What do you expect me to do?' protested Blizzard. 'Sit there and chat affably about the good times that I had with Reginald Morris?'

'Of course not, but we have to keep the media sweet. We are likely to need their help on this one. I mean, we're hardly overwhelmed by evidence, are we?'

'Yeah, but giving them the excuse to plaster Morris's face all over their front pages is hardly going to help, is it?' exclaimed Blizzard as they walked into Ronald's office. 'He's got nothing to do with this. Besides, I want to haul Les Melcham in for questioning.'

'Why? Just because he owned both houses?' said Ronald. He sat down heavily behind his desk and raised his eyes to the ceiling. 'You'll need a damned sight more than that. It'll just cause more aggravation.'

'The Super's right,' said Colley. 'We've got nothing to link him to the fires.'

'Not yet,' said Blizzard.

'These are dangerous waters,' warned Ronald. 'Remember how he threatened to sue us for wrongful arrest after you brought him in over that death? I don't want your dislike of him getting in the way of this investigation, John. I want this handled with painstaking professionalism.'

'Credit me with some intelligence, Arthur. Besides, he does not have to be behind the fires, does he? What if he's fallen out with someone and the fires are a way of putting the frighteners on Melcham?'

'He's certainly got enough enemies,' said Colley.

'All I'm asking is for permission to dig a bit deeper,' said Blizzard. He looked at Ronald. 'If only to eliminate him from our inquiries.'

'If that's all it is.' Ronald pointed his Biro at the chief inspector. 'But for heaven's sake, keep it in perspective.'

'I'll be on my best behaviour,' pledged Blizzard gravely. 'Scout's honour.'

'As I recall, the Scouts kicked you out for being a disruptive influence.'

'You'll just have to trust me then,' said Blizzard as he walked out of the office.

'What have I done?' sighed Ronald. He slumped back in his chair.

'Do the words cat and pigeons mean anything to you?' said Colley.

'Sometimes,' said Ronald, shooting the detective a withering look, 'your attempts at levity only make things worse.'

Chapter eight

Later that afternoon, it was an angry Les Melcham who paced restlessly around the foyer of Abbey Road, having heard that Blizzard would not let anyone into the fire-hit properties until the landlord had presented himself at the police station. No one summoned Les Melcham and, on arrival, he had refused to see Blizzard and demanded instead to have an audience with Arthur Ronald.

David Colley peeped through the reception grille at the landlord, a bulky man in his mid-forties whose dark suit always seemed ill-fitting. Like his colleagues, the sergeant had never liked Melcham, and now he scowled as the landlord prowled around the reception area, waiting for Ronald. Melcham was perspiring freely, the sweat beading on his brow and trickling down his puffy cheeks. From time to time, he stopped to mop his face with a grubby handkerchief. He looked worried. Colley smiled; he liked it when Les Melcham was worried.

Melcham's lawyer, on the other hand, remained calm. Paul D'Arcy always did. A tall thin-faced, beady-eyed man dressed immaculately in a dark pinstripe suit with a crisp white handkerchief of his own poking out of its breast pocket, he was no stranger to the police. Every officer had heard the stories linking him with the city's criminal fraternity; men like Les Melcham, whose apparently legitimate front as a businessman obscured an empire with tentacles that reached out across the city. Drugs, smuggled tobacco, stolen goods, protection: Les Melcham was into it all.

The sergeant chuckled as he saw a stony-faced Arthur Ronald emerge into the reception area and look without enthusiasm at Melcham. Like the rest of the police officers at Abbey Road, the superintendent made little secret of his loathing for the landlord.

'Mr Melcham,' said Ronald, trying nevertheless to sound courteous. 'I understand that you want to see me?'

'You took your time!' exclaimed Melcham angrily. 'You're Blizzard's boss. What's his fucking game?'

'I don't think for one minute…'

'Don't give me that. You know the man has got it in for me!'

As Melcham began to shout, Colley grinned and headed down the corridor towards Blizzard's office. He had heard enough. The sergeant was still smiling when he walked into the room.

'What you laughing at?' asked Blizzard, looking up from the report he was reading.

'He's still refusing to see you, and he's having a right old set-to with the Super. I should keep out of Ronald's way for a while. He looked well pissed off.'

'He'll manage. He's good at that sort of stuff, is Arthur. Did you get the gear?'

'Certainly did.' Colley sat down on the opposite side of the desk and held up a piece of paper. 'And very interesting reading it makes, too. Mind, the insurance company was a bit snotty at first. Bleating on about GDPR.'

'GD-what?'

'You not read the memos?' Colley glanced at the papers piled up in the inspector's in-tray. 'Sorry, silly question.

Anyway, their attitude improved when I told the manager that, GDPR or not, he could be charged with obstructing a police investigation.'

'I'm sure it did. So, what do they tell you?'

'You were right to be suspicious. Over the past six months, Les Melcham has increased the premiums on nine of his houses, including Inkerman and Holbrook.'

'Has he now?' Blizzard looked interested as Colley slid the piece of paper across the desk. The inspector scanned the contents. 'This says that two other houses had fires?'

'Yeah, they did, but nothing on the scale of these last two. Minor damage only. He's not claimed for Inkerman or Holbrook yet, but his claims on the two earlier ones blamed tenants dropping fags.'

'Did he give any reason for increasing his premiums?'

'Said that he had carried out improvement works which raised the value of the properties.'

'That'll be the day.'

'Indeed. When I asked the insurance company for documentation proving that the work was actually done, the manager emailed me a scan, but it didn't take much digging to find out that the papers were fake. The building company doesn't exist, for a start.'

Blizzard surveyed the printout again.

'Our friend Mr Melcham would seem to have some questions to answer, would he not? Assuming Arthur does his stuff, that is.'

At that moment, the superintendent stalked into the room.

'Ah, speak of the Devil,' said Blizzard. 'How'd it go?'

'Do what you want with the twat,' said Ronald.

'What happened to painstaking professionalism?' asked Blizzard. The inspector winked at Colley. 'I was rather hoping to learn something.'

'Painstaking professionalism, my arse.' Ronald grunted something else that neither of his colleagues caught and stumped out of the room.

Les Melcham's mood was little improved when he faced Blizzard and Colley over the table in the interview room ten minutes later. It was Paul D'Arcy who spoke first.

'Is my client under arrest?' he asked.

'Certainly not,' said Blizzard affably. 'Les is just being a good citizen and helping us with our inquiries. Pillar of the community and all that.'

'Then, as I said to your superintendent, there is nothing to keep us here another second.' D'Arcy snapped shut his briefcase and stood up.

'You're absolutely right,' said Blizzard as Melcham leered at him and also stood up. The inspector made a show of studying the document on the table. 'Of course, if your client takes one step out of this room, I'll have to arrest him on suspicion of murder.'

'Murder!' exclaimed Melcham.

'I am afraid so.'

'I ain't done no murder! And I'll take you to every court in the land if you say I have.'

'It would be a delight to actually get you into a court, Les.'

'I ain't done nothing wrong! And if you fu–'

'Please be calm, Les,' said the lawyer. He placed a restraining hand on his client's shoulder. 'You've already been threatened with a night in the cells by Superintendent Ronald for foul and abusive language, remember.'

'So, that's what he means by painstaking professionalism,' murmured Blizzard.

'I would advise you to choose your next words very carefully,' said D'Arcy. 'As I informed your superintendent, my client does not appreciate being summoned here and, given your continual harassment of him over recent times, we are very tempted to take this matter further through legal channels.'

'Cut the crap, D'Arcy. This is a murder investigation and your client may consider that, on balance, it would be wiser to stay here and have an amicable chat. Got to be better than being arrested, I would suggest.'

'I don't mind answering no questions,' said Melcham. 'He's got nothing on me.'

'I would not advise it, Les,' said his lawyer, quickly.

'He can ask what he fucking likes. I ain't got nothing to hide.'

'It seems that your client has ignored your advice,' said Blizzard with a cheerful smile. 'Now, about the fires at your houses, Les. Four in all, you really are remarkably unlucky.'

'They was accidents! I reckon the old blokes fell asleep when they was smoking.'

'Is that what your insurance claims about this weekend will say?'

'I don't know what you mean,' said Melcham. He watched uneasily as the inspector again made a point of studying the insurance documents on the desk. Fresh beads of sweat broke out on his forehead.

'Come on, Les, we're not stupid,' said Blizzard eventually. 'We rumbled the scam easily enough. It's the oldest trick in the book, increase the premiums, start a couple of fires and claim the insurance. How much were the first two payments?'

'You don't have to answer any questions about that,' said D'Arcy as his client looked worried.

'Perhaps he would rather do it under caution? Because as it stands, he is the only one with a motive to see those houses burn down. I don't think he meant for anyone to die, so we could be looking at manslaughter. What happened, Les, did it go wrong?'

'I didn't start no fires.'

'Then who did?'

'Someone else.'

'Isn't it always?' said Blizzard. 'Go on then, who do you think torched your properties?'

'Alright, if you must know…' A gleam had come into Melcham's eyes. He composed himself and dabbed his sweating forehead again with the handkerchief. 'A few months ago, I decided to expand my sphere of business operations into a couple of nightclubs, to enable them to develop their full commercial potential…'

'Cut the fancy language, Les,' said Colley. 'Everyone knows that you're running a protection racket.'

'I resent that.' Melcham glared at him. 'The point is that since I started with the clubs there have been threats against me. People who said I was on their turf.'

'Who are they?' asked Blizzard.

'I can't say. They'd have me killed if they knew I was telling you all this.'

'They can't be all bad then.' Blizzard stood up. 'OK, Les, you're free to go.'

'Just like that?' asked Melcham in astonishment.

D'Arcy looked surprised as well, as did Colley.

'Just like that,' said Blizzard.

'What if I gave you some names?'

'No, it's alright,' said Blizzard as he headed for the door. 'Just don't leave town, there's a good chap.'

'Are we to get a fuller explanation?' asked D'Arcy. He could not conceal his irritation that Blizzard had taken control of the situation.

'No.' Blizzard held open the door. 'Now, get out before I change my mind and lock you both up.'

'I would just like to say,' said D'Arcy, standing up, 'that your attitude throughout this interview has been disgraceful, Chief Inspector, and I shall be writing to the chief constable in the strongest terms.'

'You do that. David, see Mr D'Arcy and his slime-ball client off the premises, please.'

D'Arcy and Melcham stalked angrily from the room, and the chief inspector headed the other way down the corridor. A couple of minutes later, Colley hurried into the chief inspector's office.

'What are you playing at?' he demanded. 'We were getting somewhere.'

'No, we weren't. There haven't been any threats. Didn't you see his eyes light up when he realised that us investigating threats against him could add legitimacy to his insurance claim? Probably made it up on the spur of the moment. He's a cunning bastard.'

'Surely we're not letting it drop?'

'Of course, we're not. Give me some credit. Check with Elaine Harrison at the fire brigade. See if she agrees that the last two fires were down to someone else. Oh, and track down the insurance man who arranged his dodgy policies.'

'I'll get on it. Ronald's not going to be very pleased when he hears about Melcham's letter, mind.'

'That's Mr Ronald to you,' said the superintendent, entering the room and fixing the sergeant with a stare. 'What letter?'

Colley said nothing but looked at Blizzard.

'Paul D'Arcy is going to write to the governor expressing his high regard for the painstakingly professional way I am handling the investigation,' said the inspector. He lowered his voice. 'Keep it to yourself, Arthur, but I think he might be about to recommend me for a medal.'

'Brilliant.' Ronald sighed. 'That's all we need. Where is he now?'

'I let him go. I suspect Les Melcham of most things but, much as it galls me to say it, it doesn't sound right. Maybe for the first two, but these last two... Don't think so.'

'So, what are our alternatives?' asked Ronald.

'We've either got someone with a grudge against both Pembridge and Lowther, or some sicko who just likes starting fires for the hell of it.'

'In which case…' said Ronald gravely. He held up the brown envelope he was carrying. 'You might like to open this.'

'Not sure I do,' said Blizzard.

'Is it another one?' asked Colley.

The chief inspector pulled out a single sheet of white paper and scanned the handwritten contents.

'I'm afraid so,' he said. 'It says "You are of a world that has not learned to learn. Now she has burst forth and you have seen her fiery swathe. This is their Hell on earth".'

Blizzard placed the piece of paper on the desk.

'I want this checking out, David,' he said. 'I know the last one was clean, but I want forensics to give it the once over anyway. And it's a local postmark so I want to find out if there is any way that Reginald Morris could have mailed it.'

'But you said it yourself, he's been locked up for twenty years.'

'Yeah, but I would dearly love to know if Crake Lane ever lets him out for the day.'

And without a further word, John Blizzard stood up and walked from the room, his footsteps echoing down the deserted corridor.

Ronald picked up the desk phone.

'Something tells me that this crackpot is going to try again,' he said. 'I think we're going to have to increase our uniform patrols. Engage in a spot of public reassurance. Which reminds me, Sergeant, what are you doing tonight?'

Chapter nine

'I still don't see why Arthur thinks I have to go with you,' said David Colley as he eased his vehicle out of the car park that evening.

'So that you can shuffle papers importantly and trot out some useful statistics if I get stuck,' said Blizzard. 'Falling crime, that kind of malarkey.'

'You know it's going to be a bear-pit, I take it?'

'I fear you are right.'

Blizzard was not looking forward to the event at a church hall not far from Inkerman Street. Every day, his job brought him into contact with the sordid underbelly of city life but, despite the procession of evil characters who occupied his time, there was one task above all others which he dreaded – being ordered by Arthur Ronald to address a Police Consultative Forum meeting. The forums had been the idea of the new Assistant Chief Constable, who had arrived with a raft of initiatives to, as he kept saying, 'make Hafton police more accountable'. Blizzard regarded them as an unnecessary diversion and that night, which had been in the diary for months, promised to be particularly testing.

Colley guided the car into the early evening traffic.

'I take it you know that they'll want to talk about the fires?' said the sergeant. 'Not sure we can offer much reassurance there.'

He adopted a nasal voice. 'In 2017 nobody died, in 2018 nobody died, in 2019 two people died.'

He noticed the inspector's bemused expression.

'It's a Steve Coogan character.'

'I'm not really in the mood for jokes. I have got better things to do tonight,' Blizzard said.

'*You've* got better things to do. I'd hoped you might let me get away for rugby practice. Hey, fancy some music to cheer us up on the way?'

Without waiting for an answer, the sergeant reached forward, flicked a switch, and energetic rock music filled the car.

'What the hell is that?' asked Blizzard with a grimace.

'The Prodigy. You'll like this album. It's got a track called *Firestarter* on it.'

'Just drive the car,' said Blizzard. 'And switch this bloody racket off.'

Colley grinned but did as he was told. A few minutes later, they pulled up outside the church, a grimy Victorian building with crumbling brickwork. Nearby stood the recently built single-storey church hall.

'How the hell can they afford that?' said Blizzard.

'Donations.'

'Who said the church is broke?'

'It is now,' said Colley as they got out of the car. 'Someone got into the safe and nicked all their money a few nights ago. Sarah Allatt's looking at it, but no luck so far. I suspect they'll be more interested in that than the fires.'

'Brilliant,' said Blizzard. He turned on a smile and extended a hand as the vicar approached up the drive. 'Good evening, Reverend.'

'Good evening, gentlemen,' said the vicar, shaking their hands vigorously. 'I don't suppose you've got the little beggars who broke into our safe?'

''Fraid not,' said Blizzard.

'Ah well, we live in hope,' said the vicar. 'Anyway, I hope you have girded your loins as there are at least a hundred people in there, all with questions to ask you. They're very worried about these fires, you know.'

'I'm sure they are, Reverend. Lead on.'

'Into the lion's den, eh?' quipped the vicar.

Blizzard gave him a bleak look and the clergyman ushered the detectives into the hall, which was packed with people gazing at them expectantly.

'Next time,' muttered Blizzard, taking a seat at the front and surveying the sea of faces, 'Ronald does this one.'

Only he heard Colley's low voice murmuring 'In 2017…' as he sat down next to his boss.

After a few preambles, the vicar turned to the detectives.

'Well, gentlemen,' he said, 'I am sure that people have plenty of questions to ask. Who would like to be first? Yes, man at the back. In the dark suit.'

'Brilliant,' said Blizzard as he recognised the man who had stood up.

Colley covered his mouth with a hand to hide the smile.

'As a local businessman,' said the questioner, 'I am very worried about the recent arson attacks. I think I speak for a lot of people here when I say that we would feel a lot safer if the police had not reduced the number of uniformed officers patrolling the streets over recent months. Law-abiding citizens like us deserve better.'

A smattering of applause ran round the hall.

'This could be one of those nights,' Blizzard muttered. He stood up. 'Thank you for the question, Mr Melcham. It is Mr Melcham, isn't it?'

* * *

'Hello, what's this?' said Blizzard as Colley guided the car through the night-time streets towards a series of flashing blue lights.

It was shortly after 9.30pm and, the police forum having finished, the detectives were on their way to Abbey Road Police Station. Neither man had spoken since they had left the church; the meeting had proved to be a bruising encounter. The sergeant pulled the car up alongside the wasteland beyond the complex of railway lines running out of the city centre railway station, and the officers got out.

'This is near your engine shed, isn't it?' asked the sergeant.

'Over there.' Blizzard wafted a hand across the wasteland, over which they could see pinpricks of torchlight as uniformed officers searched the site. Blizzard spotted an inspector standing by one of the police cars and walked over.

'What's happening?' he asked. 'They're not after our shed, are they?'

'Dunno. A member of the public rang in to report someone carrying a can of petrol.' The inspector watched as one of the uniformed officers walked over. 'Anything?'

'False alarm. A couple of the lads found the guy over by Rocket Street. Turns out his car had run out of petrol.'

'It's been like this ever since the fires,' said the inspector. 'People are very jumpy. This is the fifth report we've had tonight, John. The sooner you get him...'

He did not finish the sentence but gestured instead for his officers to abandon the search. As they left the wasteland and returned to their vehicles, a woman in her thirties walked up to Blizzard.

'What's happening?' she asked.

'Just routine inquiries,' said the inspector. 'Nothing to worry about.'

'Is it to do with the arsonist?'

'I am afraid I cannot–'

'All these police officers, it must be. It's very like what happened with Reginald Morris, isn't it?'

Blizzard was about to give a sharp retort but noticed that tears had started to glisten in her eyes.

'Why do you say that?' he asked.

'My aunt was one of his victims.' Her voice was quiet now. 'She did not stand a chance. I was in the next bedroom when the fire started. The firefighters rescued me.'

'I'm sorry about—'

'Just get whoever is doing it this time.' She gripped his arm. 'No one should go through what we went through. This is bringing back a lot of awful memories for people.'

She turned and walked away. A pensive Blizzard watched her go, then glanced across the wasteland. He looked at Colley.

'Mind if I check the shed?' he said.

Colley shook his head and he followed the inspector across the wasteland to a corrugated iron shed. Blizzard produced a key from his jacket pocket, opened the creaking door and flicked the light switch. In front of them, surrounded by pieces of scrap metal and old tools, dimly illuminated by the light of a stark single light bulb, was an old railway engine, the burnished coppering of the rust on her sides testament to years of neglect. For Colley, fastening his anorak against the evening chill, it looked nothing more than a lump of junk but he knew that, for John Blizzard, it was a thing of beauty.

'This is the new one, is it?' asked Colley. 'Not much to look at, is it?'

'She's a she, David. Gas Board Number Sixteen.' Blizzard looked lovingly at the steam engine. The son of a train driver, he had several years previously founded the Hafton Railway Appreciation Society, a small group of enthusiastic like-minded individuals who renovated steam engines. 'Haven't been down here for weeks, what with work and the baby. I do my best thinking here.'

'And what are you thinking now?'

Blizzard looked worried.

'I am thinking,' he said, 'that those people at that meeting tonight were depending on us to ease their fears, as was that woman whose aunt died – but we couldn't offer them anything. Forget Les Melcham playing his silly games, people are scared and I didn't know what to say to them. I don't like it.'

The inspector startled his sergeant with an uncharacteristic burst of anger as he slammed a fist into the side of the locomotive.

'We'll get the break we need,' said Colley. 'We've got a good team working on it.'

Blizzard did not reply but led the way out of the shed. Once he had locked the gate, he paused to look across at the orange streetlights on the far side of the wasteland.

'He's out there somewhere, David,' he said quietly. 'And we're no nearer to him than the moment he got into Albert Pembridge's flat.'

'We'll get him,' repeated Colley.

'Yes, but how many times will he kill before we do?' Blizzard started walking towards the car, his feet crunching on broken glass. 'Because if there's one thing you can guarantee about arsonists, it's that they keep going until you stop them. Reginald Morris killed eight. He'd have killed eight more if we'd let him.'

'Yes, but he's nothing to–'

'I'll be honest, David, this guy has got me rattled.'

Colley looked at his boss with concern. In the chief inspector's eyes was a strange look he had not seen before. Colley cast round for the best description. Reluctantly, he settled on 'fear.' The sergeant shivered. And it wasn't because he was cold.

Chapter ten

The next day dawned gloomy, the rain having fallen remorselessly overnight so that the police station car park was covered in puddles and the trees dripped steadily outside Blizzard's office window. The chief inspector had arrived early, driven from his bed by another vivid nightmare in which he was again plunged into the crackling fires of the burning city – only this time, he was one of the thousands fleeing for their lives. Every time he reached the end of a street, his way was blocked by a small, stooped figure whose face was obscured by shadow, but which he did not need to see to recognise. When the face was finally exposed, flames sent ghostly shapes dancing across its glinting eyes and leering lips, which were pulled back to expose crooked, stained teeth. The sight of Reginald Morris after so many years had jerked Blizzard awake, and for a few moments he lay there, his body running with sweat, heart thumping.

Now, Blizzard was sitting with his feet propped up on the desk, staring out at the rain, when his phone rang. Without lowering his feet to the floor, he reached out and picked up the receiver.

'Is that John Blizzard?' said a woman's voice.

'The very same.'

'This is Elaine Harrison at the fire brigade. Your sergeant asked me to check out the earlier fires at the houses owned by Les Melcham.'

'He did indeed. What did you find?'

'They're totally different. A different method of ignition, for starters. The earlier ones were started with burning rags pushed through the letterbox. They didn't cause much damage at all.'

'But could the last two have been started by the same person? Maybe disappointed at the scale of the earlier ones?'

'Anything's possible, I suppose, but my experience is that arsonists like to stick with their tried and trusted methods. The most recent ones were very different. I've emailed the details through to David.'

Five minutes later, call finished, the inspector was still sitting with his feet on the desk when the office door opened and Colley appeared. He had a couple of pieces of paper in his hand.

'They said you'd been in from early,' he said. 'Still bothered about last night?'

'Yeah, couldn't sleep. And when I did drop off, all I saw was Reginald Morris laughing at me. Can't get him out of my mind, David. The killings have all his hallmarks. It's uncanny.'

'Yeah, but he's still banged up. I checked with Crake Lane last night.'

'See,' said Blizzard with a knowing smile, 'he's got you at it now.'

'I did it to put your mind at rest so you can concentrate properly. Crake Lane told me that, although he is allowed out on occasion, he's always supervised. There has not been a moment when Reginald Morris has been out on his own since he went there.'

'I know, but the more I think about it, the more I am convinced that somebody is copying him.'

'But who? It was twenty years ago. It's ancient history.'

'When you're my age, you'll thank people not to refer to twenty years ago as ancient history,' said Blizzard. 'Besides, I'm not the only one in this city for whom those events are not ancient history. They're living it every day. That woman last night, for example; and Control have received several calls from people just like her.'

'Yes, I know but…'

'And there's been enough written about him over the past two decades to keep the memories alive. Every other pulp crime book that comes out seems to mention him, and Channel 5 did that documentary to mark the twentieth anniversary, remember. Besides, he's met enough crackerjacks in Crake Lane over the past twenty years. What if one of them has been released and is trying to be the next Reginald Morris?'

'I suppose it's always a possibility, but I checked and no one fits the bill. If you want my opinion, you're letting Reginald Morris cloud your judgment.'

Colley held his breath and watched for a reaction. You never quite knew how Blizzard would respond to criticism and, although the two men had a strong relationship, that did not mean that the sergeant could say what he liked. Blizzard did not seem angry, though.

'Then what about these?' he said. He took the letters out of his desk drawer. 'Someone sent them, didn't they?'

'I didn't say that we should disregard the idea altogether. In fact, Sarah suggested she take copies round bookshops in the city, to see if anyone recognises the writing style. Personally, I only think she did it to get away from the vicar and his blessed safe. He was on the phone at ten past eight this morning.'

'Best find the toerag that nicked the cash, then.'

'Indeed. However, I've got something else that we can get our teeth into first.'

'So have I,' said Blizzard. 'Elaine Harrison has just been on. Reckons the first two fires at Melcham's place were a totally different MO.'

'I know.' Colley held up the computer printouts in his hand. 'And I know someone who might be able to tell us a bit more. Melcham's insurance policies were handled by the guy who runs the branch office in Hafton. A chap called George Ferris. I asked around and it seems that our Mr Ferris is deeply in debt to a local moneylender. It's all got a bit heavy, by all accounts... and guess who the moneylender is?'

'Not The Royal Bank of Melcham, by any chance?'

'The very same.'

'Excellent work, David,' said Blizzard. Finally, he lowered his feet from the desk. 'Come on, let's bring Ferris in.'

* * *

An hour later, it was an uneasy George Ferris who sat opposite the two stern-faced detectives in the interview room. One look at the frightened expression on the insurance man's face had been enough to convince the officers that he was not a willing partner in the criminal enterprise in which he had become embroiled. Now, Ferris, a wiry man with bony cheeks, greying hair and wearing spectacles, stared with trepidation across the table at the officers.

'So,' said Blizzard. 'How did you fall into the clutches of a slimeball like Les Melcham?'

'Online poker.' Ferris shook his head. 'Ran up debts of more than five grand. I don't know how, but Melcham found out and offered to lend me the money.'

'And when you couldn't pay the interest, he persuaded you to set up the scam with the insurance policies on his houses?'

'Hang on, I thought I was here to talk about illegal moneylending? I know nothing about any insurance scam, and if you–'

'Oh, don't play games with us, George,' said Blizzard. 'I really am not in the mood. I want to know everything about Les Melcham's insurance scam, and I want to know it now.'

'I can't,' whispered Ferris. Beads of sweat sprang up on his forehead. 'He'll kill me if I talk.'

'And I'll have you for murder if you don't.'

'Murder!' gasped Ferris in horror. 'But I haven't done any murders!'

'Were not the houses in Inkerman Street and Holbrook Street covered by the new policies?'

'Yes, but they weren't supposed to be the ones that...' Ferris's voice tailed off. 'I'm saying nothing more.'

'I think you've said quite enough already. In fact, I've half a mind to charge you as an accessory to murder right now.'

'You're bluffing.'

'Sergeant!' snapped Blizzard. Colley leaned forward.

'OK, OK,' said Ferris. 'I'll tell you. It was Les's idea.'

'Now tell me something I don't know.'

'He threatened to hurt my wife and the children.' Tears started to run down Ferris's cheeks. 'I had no alternative. My family mean everything to me.'

'Almost as much as the gee-gees,' said Blizzard. 'So, tell me, what exactly did he want you to do?'

'He said he would wipe out the debt if I got him increased premiums on some of his houses.'

'Including Holbrook and Inkerman?'

'Yeah. And the other ones where there were fires. The earlier ones.'

Colley glanced at the pieces of paper lying on the desk.

'Matthew Street and German Street?' he asked.

'Yeah, that's them. He knew my firm would demand proof that the buildings had been improved, so he made me fake the documentation. It was easy to get his claims accepted on the first two fires. No one queried them.'

'Well, it'll not be so easy now,' said Blizzard.

'I didn't know that anyone would die.' Ferris buried his head in his hands, shoulders heaving as the sobs wracked his body. Eventually, he looked up at them, the tears streaming across his cheeks. 'You have to believe me.'

'Do you know who started the fires?' asked Colley.

Ferris shook his head.

'No,' he said. 'And that's the God's honest truth.'

* * *

Twenty minutes later, the interview at an end and Ferris bailed pending further enquiries, the detectives made their way to Ronald's office, where Blizzard took a seat at the desk and Colley leaned against the wall.

'So, it's a good old-fashioned insurance job, then?' said Ronald.

'That's what it looks like, sure,' said Blizzard.

'But I sense you're not convinced?'

'Not about the murders, no. I think Ferris is telling the truth, but the first fires were different, much smaller. Melcham got paid insurance for both of them so he had no need to escalate things. Les Melcham may be many things but he's not stupid. He knows that two old guys dying on successive nights would have us swarming all over him – and he must have known that it wouldn't take us long to rumble the insurance scam.'

'Unless nobody was supposed to die,' said Colley. 'Perhaps everyone was supposed to get out and it went wrong.'

'Except that anyone with any sense would start the fires a longer time apart to reduce suspicion,' said Blizzard. 'I mean, two in two nights? Give me a break.'

'So, what now?' asked Ronald.

'We turn a few stones over and see what crawls out. We can pull Les Melcham in any time we want. He's not going anywhere.'

'Makes sense,' said Ronald. 'In the meantime, the chief constable has agreed to continued high level patrols in the area.'

'The man has clearly got a strong sense of history.'

'What do you mean?'

'One of his predecessors did the same thing for Reginald Morris.' Blizzard stood up and headed out into the corridor. 'And look what happened there...'

Chapter eleven

The breakthrough that Blizzard desperately needed came late that afternoon from Sarah Allatt, a slim brunette who had recently been appointed as one of Western CID's detective constables and who had spent the day trudging round the city's bookshops in the rain. Her last stop as the light started to fade was in a back street not far from the university. Entering the dingy shop, her arrival heralded by the feeble wheeze of an old bell, she was struck by the musty aroma. The detective held up her warrant card so that the bespectacled, grey-haired man behind the counter could see.

'I take it you are here on official business?' he said.

Allatt nodded, took the photocopy of the poem from her handbag and passed it over the counter.

'Do you recognise this?' she asked.

He peered at it over the top of his spectacles.

'It's by Raymond Marriott, if I'm not mistaken,' he said. 'I recognise the style.'

The shop owner walked round from behind the counter and over to a shelf bearing a faded handwritten label which said 'Poetry'. He ran his hand along the books before eventually taking down a slim volume, which he handed to the detective.

'It's in there, I believe,' he said.

Allatt flicked through the pages and found the poem.

'I've never heard of him,' she said, looking up. 'Is he famous?'

'He's no Simon Armitage.'

'Who?'

'Not a fan of poetry, then?'

'Not really.'

'Suffice to say that Raymond Marriott is one of the more obscure Northern poets. Lives out on the coast. A cottage outside Rawnsea, I think. Bit of a recluse, although he did pop in a few weeks back. Just for a couple of minutes. He's bringing out a new collection. His first in five years. Can I ask what this is about?'

'Just routine inquiries. Can I keep the book?'

'Only if you pay for it,' said the shopkeeper. 'I'll take a tenner, since it's you.'

'What, a tenner for that? I'm not sure it's even fifty pages!'

'I told you he was obscure. He only produced a hundred or so, and it's been out of print for years.'

Allatt sighed and wondered what Accounts would make of the purchase on her expenses sheet.

* * *

The next morning, Allatt picked up John Blizzard from outside Abbey Road Police Station. It was the first time she had worked just with the DCI, and she had slept little the previous night. An ambitious young officer keen to make her mark following her transfer from uniform to Western CID, she was anticipating the experience with a mixture of excitement and trepidation. Everyone knew that working with Blizzard could be a challenge.

After an hour's drive, in which little was said, Allatt parked her car at the end of a bumpy track, and she and

Blizzard walked towards the writer's clifftop cottage, the sun bright in their eyes and the breeze blowing hard and salty off the North Sea.

The cottage door was opened by a tall, thin man in his mid-fifties, his fair hair receding and tied back in a ponytail and his narrow eyes hidden by tinted gold-rimmed glasses. He was dressed in a chunky green sweater, scuffed black cords and open-toed sandals.

'Raymond Marriott?' said Blizzard.

'Who wants to know?'

The detective flashed his warrant card.

'I am Detective Chief Inspector John Blizzard,' he said. 'And this is Detective Constable Allatt. We are conducting a murder investigation and we believe you may be able to help us.'

'You had better come in, then,' said Marriott. He gestured them into the cottage. 'Although quite why you wish to talk to me, I am not sure.'

The living room was sparsely furnished; in one corner stood a rickety table on which was a pen and a blank sheet of paper, in another, several wooden boxes were stacked; on top of them was a lobster pot, against which was propped a fishing rod. In the centre of the room stood a small threadbare grey settee and two ramshackle chairs.

'You must excuse my lack of home comforts,' said the poet. He sat on the sofa and gestured to the chairs. 'Poetry is a poor man's game, I am afraid. Now, how can I help you?'

'There have been two arsons in Hafton.' Blizzard took a seat. 'Two elderly men died.'

'And?'

'This is from one of your poems, I think.' Blizzard reached into his jacket pocket and produced the photocopy of the handwritten verses that had been sent to him. He handed them over. 'The constable here tracked it down to one of your books.'

'It is one of mine, yes,' said the writer after studying the piece. 'A somewhat old poem. Where did you get this?'

'Possibly from the killer.'

'One can never legislate for those whom one's poetry touches,' murmured Marriott. 'But any number of people could have confirmed that I wrote it. Why come all this way to see me?'

'We need to eliminate you from our inquiries,' said Blizzard.

'Eliminate me? Just because I wrote the poem does not mean that I would put into practice its sentiments, Chief Inspector.'

'The poem was posted in the city. Do you go into Hafton at all?'

'Just to kill people.'

'Just answer the question.'

'Why should I?' exclaimed Marriott. 'This is ridiculous. It is exactly the reason I live out here. Our modern society has become so infected with—'

'Cut the philosophy,' said Blizzard.

'As you wish,' replied the poet, coldly. 'To answer your question, I try not to visit the city unless I really have to. Unfortunately, though, my works are not commercially attractive to publishers, so I am forced to finance their publication myself, then hawk my wares round bookshops, rather like a common prostitute. Indeed, I am intrigued that you recognised the poem. Don't tell me that my work is favoured bedtime reading for police officers these days?'

'The bookseller in Portland Street recognised it,' said Allatt. 'He sold us a copy of the book. That's how we know about you. Up until then, we did not even know you existed.'

'Such is the price of obscurity,' said Marriott with a sigh. 'Although, I'm very big in Holland. I lived there for the best part of twenty years.'

'The bookseller also said that you are bringing out a new collection,' said Allatt.

'Bless him. He is one of the few booksellers in the city who stocks my work – the university students, you see.'

'Students?' asked Blizzard, suddenly interested. He thought back to Andy Hemmings. 'They buy your work?'

'They do. It has assumed what you might call cult status with some of the young people on the English Literature course. Last year, the university even invited me to give a seminar. Interestingly enough, one of the poems I read was this one that was sent to you.'

'It is interesting,' said Blizzard. 'Very interesting, indeed. What exactly does the poem mean?'

'I have long held the belief that each one of us possesses great power which, in some cases, wells to the surface and consumes all about it.'

'Like fire.'

'I didn't kill them, Chief Inspector.'

'But can you say the same about your words?' said Blizzard. He stood up. 'Think about that.'

'We can never be sure who they touch,' said the poet. 'And in what way they influence our readers.'

'Indeed. Good day, Mr Marriott.'

Marriott showed no emotion as he watched the detectives leave the cottage. Blizzard was about to swing himself into the car when a thought struck him and he glanced back at the writer, who was leaning against the door frame and surveying them in thoughtful silence.

'Tell me!' shouted the chief inspector. 'Have you ever visited Crake Lane Hospital?'

'My poems may not be everybody's cup of tea,' shouted the poet with a slight smile, 'but they're not that bad.'

'That's quite witty,' said Allatt.

'Just drive the car,' said Blizzard.

The inspector got into the vehicle and stared moodily out of the window as Allatt pulled away, resolving to keep her mouth shut next time. As Colley had warned her the previous evening, you could never be sure which way it would go with John Blizzard. She rebuked herself silently, cursing her over-confidence. Noticing her worried expression, Blizzard shot her a half-smile.

'And, yes,' he said, 'it was quite funny. But if you ever tell Raymond Marriott, I may have to kill you.'

Allatt heaved a sigh of relief and laughed. Blizzard resumed his staring out of the window. Allatt could not see it but he was still smiling; oh, how he loved having a reputation.

Chapter twelve

Professor Leonard Wright, a high-browed bespectacled man in his mid-fifties, set the tray down on the desk.

'Should I be mother?' he asked, looking at Blizzard and Allatt.

They were in the Head of English Literature's tiny book-lined office on the top floor of the tower block, one of two unsightly concrete blocks constructed in the 1980s when the university required more space to house extra students.

'Did either of you attend the university?' asked the academic. He poured out the tea from a china pot, then sat down.

Allatt nodded.

'I got a first in History,' she said.

'Excellent, excellent. And you, Chief Inspector?'

'I joined the police straight from school. I wasn't a particularly brilliant student, I am afraid.'

'Which school in the city did you attend?'

'Actually, I grew up in rural Lincolnshire.' Blizzard took a sip of tea. 'We only came here when my father was transferred. He was a train driver. I was fifteen at the time.'

'It must be difficult working in a city like Hafton after knowing country life as you did.'

'I've got used to it – except the rain, that is. Not sure you ever get used to the rain in Hafton.'

'Indeed. However, I don't imagine you came here to talk about the weather, Chief Inspector. How can I help?'

'You have probably heard that we are investigating a double murder. Two elderly men were burnt to death in streets not far from here. Arson.'

'Ah, yes, I did hear something of that. One of my final year students lives in the house where one of the fires occurred; a young man by the name of Andy Hemmings. Pleasant fellow.'

'And very courageous. He tried to save one of the old men.'

'He did not mention that, but then I would not have expected him to have done so. He's a very modest, quiet young man, is Andy Hemmings. You say these fires were deliberate?'

'As far as we can ascertain.'

'What a terrible thing to happen.' Wright shook his head. 'Man's inhumanity to man never ceases to amaze me. But how on earth can I help you?'

Blizzard glanced at Allatt, who held up the photocopy.

'We have received a copy of a poem sent to us by the person we believe to be the killer,' said the constable. She passed the piece of paper to the professor. 'It is by a writer called Marriott...'

'Raymond Marriott, yes,' said the professor. 'He delivered a lecture here last year.'

'Why did you invite him?' asked Blizzard.

'Our last inspection suggested that our curriculum is somewhat mainstream and I have been attempting to extend its range to include more modern works.'

'Why Raymond Marriott?'

'I thought that an obscure Northern poet might allow us to tick a box or two. I rather wish I hadn't.'

'Why?'

'Not a man I liked, Chief Inspector. A somewhat abrupt, ill-mannered character. Arrogant, I thought.'

'What about his poetry?' asked Allatt. She took the anthology out of her bag and held it up. 'Any good?'

'Not really, although he does have what we might describe as a cult following among some of the students.' The professor reached for a biscuit. 'His work does contain a passion lacking in many other people's works. Certainly, a number of the patients seemed to appreciate it.'

'Patients?' asked Blizzard sharply.

'Yes, at Crake Lane.'

'You read Marriott's poetry at Crake Lane?'

'The hospital invited us to stage poetry recitals. We did a couple last year.' Wright looked pleased with himself. 'They were most successful. Young Andy Hemmings was among the students who went, as I recall.'

'Why, in God's name, would Crake Lane want you to read poetry to the patients?' asked Blizzard. He shook his head in astonishment. 'It just puts ideas into their heads.'

'Mental health awareness has made great strides, Chief Inspector. It's part of their therapy. And, from our point of view, it allows us to put something back into the community. I was rather surprised, actually. Some of the patients were remarkably knowledgeable. There's even one old chap there who writes his own poetry. Now what was his name... it's on the tip of my tongue...'

'Reginald Morris,' said Blizzard quietly.

'That's the chap. How do you know that?'

Blizzard felt a rising nausea in the pit of his stomach.

'You've never heard of Reginald Morris?' he asked.

'I am afraid not.'

'But he's notorious in Hafton.'

'I only came to the university a year or so ago. Should I have heard of him? Is there anything wrong in what we did?'

'Surely, the hospital told you why Morris is in there?'

'Their background is never discussed.' Wright looked anxious. 'Is there a problem? It's just that we are due back next month.'

'I would earnestly suggest that you don't go.' Blizzard drained his cup and stood up.

'Why ever not?'

'Because Reginald Morris and Raymond Marriott share an unhealthy fascination with fire. In fact, that's how Morris killed his victims.'

'Oh dear.' The academic went pale. 'You don't think that our readings could have anything to do with these killings, do you?'

'You had better hope not.' Blizzard opened the office door. 'Because you would have difficulty explaining that to the inspectors, wouldn't you?'

And he and Allatt left the shocked professor sitting in horrified silence in his book-lined office at the top of his ivory tower.

Chapter thirteen

'You want to do what?' exclaimed Ronald.

'I want to interview Reginald Morris,' replied Blizzard calmly.

'But he's been locked up for twenty years.' Ronald fixed his chief inspector with a stern look across his desk. 'I hope you've got a good reason, because this will need authorisation and you're hardly flavour of the month with the chief constable.'

'I never am. Besides, you know that I would not suggest it without good reason.'

'And what does your sergeant think about it?' Ronald looked across the desk at Colley.

'Well, until the governor got back from the university, I'd have said the only reason he needed to go to Crake Lane was for treatment.'

'Not exactly the unqualified support I might have expected from my loyal sergeant,' murmured Blizzard.

'But now there does seem to be good reason to interview Morris.'

'So, convince me.' Ronald sat back in his chair, crossed his arms and fixed the chief inspector with an expectant stare.

'The person who sent the letters quoted from the work of Raymond Marriott, an obscure poet read by a small number of people but popular among students at the university. Last year, Marriott conducted a seminar there, followed by a reading of his work at Crake Lane. Reginald Morris was in the audience.'

'It hardly constitutes grounds for...'

'One of the students who visited Crake Lane was Andy Hemmings, the lad who tried to rescue Bill Lowther from the fire. He's an English Literature student at the university.'

'You fancy him?' Ronald perked up as he saw the first sign of something that he could use to reassure a worried chief constable. 'Is he a suspect?'

'I would not go that far yet,' replied Blizzard. 'But our inquiries show that he is an impressionable young man. Perhaps Marriott's poetry put a few ideas into his head. Perhaps he even met Reginald Morris during the recital at Crake Lane.'

'Has this Hemmings lad got a record?' asked the superintendent.

'Only minor stuff.' Colley looked at a piece of paper he was holding. 'Couple of cautions for possession of cannabis when he was sixteen, and last year he was fined for riding his motorcycle without a crash helmet.'

'Hardly the actions of a serial killer,' said Ronald. 'I mean, you've got no motive for starters.'

'Do we need one?' asked Blizzard. 'Reginald Morris's only motive was that he liked setting fire to things because the voices in his head told him to do it. What if this Hemmings lad hears them as well?'

'It's interesting, I'll give you that, but I am still not convinced. And if the media get hold of it... I mean, think of the headlines.'

'We'll just have to make sure they don't.'

'Nevertheless...'

'Besides, do we really have a choice?' said Blizzard. His voice had assumed an urgency and the words came out in a rush. 'The people at that meeting last night were worried as hell, Arthur; the control room is being inundated with calls and we bumped into a woman who damn near died in a fire started by Reginald Morris. She is terrified that history is repeating itself. Jesus, *I* am terrified that history is repeating itself.'

'Yeah,' said Colley, 'and there's all sorts of wild speculation on Facebook. And if you look at *The Daily Herald*'s website, Gary Mistry virtually said that we're looking for a copycat.'

'I will not have police tactics dictated by *The*—'

'I know this means sticking our necks out,' said Blizzard, cutting across the superintendent. 'But if there is even the faintest chance that there is a link, we have to check it out, surely? We owe it to the people of this city. If it wasn't Reginald Morris, we wouldn't even be having this conversation. We'd have already interviewed him.'

Ronald looked at the determined expression on the inspector's face, nodded, picked up the telephone and dialled an internal number.

'Irene, get me the chief constable, please,' he said. 'Tell him it's urgent... tell him I want to discuss poetry. Yes, you heard me right, poetry. The boy stood on the burning deck, that sort of thing.'

'Thank you,' said Blizzard. 'Although I'm not sure that's the poem I'd have chosen.'

For the first time in what seemed a long time, Arthur Ronald allowed himself to smile.

* * *

Shortly after midnight, the man guided his car past the large houses set back from the wide, tree-lined roads which picked their way through the affluent western fringes of the city. He turned into Lodge Park Avenue and brought the vehicle to a halt outside The Cedars – a nursing home for the elderly built in the 1970s and set in its own wooded grounds. The man sat for a few moments, staring at the building. There were plenty of downstairs lights on, and he could see through the frosted glass the shadowy shapes of members of staff moving about.

He had just cut the engine and settled down to wait for the home to quieten down when he glanced at his rear-view mirror as a set of headlights appeared at the far end of the road. Looking closer, he could see that they belonged to a police patrol vehicle which was driving slowly towards him. The man gave a sharp intake of breath, fighting back panic, but the patrol vehicle stopped outside one of the houses further down the road and two officers got out and walked up the drive. The man slipped the car into gear, switched on the lights and drove off into the night. The next victim would have to wait.

Chapter fourteen

Crake Lane maximum security mental hospital, which stood in open countryside, prided itself on the humane and constructive care of its patients. Pleasantly furnished single-storey accommodation blocks were linked by tree-lined paths and surrounded by flower beds, neatly manicured lawns and sports fields. The regime was relaxed, with patients allowed to wear their own clothes and walk round the grounds during daytime, mingling freely with hospital staff.

Reginald Morris had lived there for two decades. Like many of the residents, he had been sent to Crake Lane by the courts with a recommendation that he only be released when it was certain that he no longer posed a risk to the public. No one thought that would ever apply to the hospital's most infamous occupant. Morris had never shown any remorse for a three-year reign of terror during which he started thirteen fires and claimed the lives of five women and three men, all elderly and living in terraced streets on the edge of the city centre.

Morris was only arrested when the police got lucky. And he was apprehended by the man who now locked up his vehicle in the car park and walked towards the main entrance. The young John Blizzard had briefly become a reluctant media star when, driving home after work at 11.30pm one evening, he spotted a man acting suspiciously on wasteland, stopped him, and discovered that he was carrying a petrol can. The city's biggest ever manhunt was over.

'Aren't you worried about meeting him again?' asked Colley, as the officers walked across the car park.

'I don't know how I feel,' said Blizzard.

But he did. A week after Morris was sentenced, Blizzard had received a poem with an attached note describing how he would one day kill the detective. During what became a highly successful career, Blizzard shrugged off many such threats, but the one from Reginald Morris stayed with him, lurking in the recesses of his mind.

'Do you think he might be tempted to have a go at you when we get to see him?' asked Colley.

'No. He's a coward – all arsonists are.'

'And you haven't seen him since you arrested him?'

'Only when he was sentenced. I can still remember the gasp that went round that courtroom when the judge sent him to Crake Lane.'

'Folks thought he should have gone to prison?'

'Yeah, and so did I. And, more importantly, so did the families of his victims. There were people in tears.'

'But the shrinks said he was mad.'

'They did, but the officers on the investigation team were livid. They thought he had hammed it up, invented the voices, conned the doctors. He's as sane as you or me.'

The automatic door to the reception area slid smoothly open and soon the detectives were being led through a corridor to an office in which sat a slim, clean-shaven man in his thirties with neatly groomed short brown hair, smartly dressed in a dark suit.

'Take a seat, gentlemen,' said hospital administrator Martin Hayley. He leaned over his tidy desk and extended a welcoming hand. 'I don't believe we have met before.

Perhaps you would like a cup of tea or coffee before we start?'

'No thanks,' said Blizzard. 'All I want is Morris.'

'I have to say that your request is somewhat irregular, Chief Inspector. Am I permitted to know exactly why you wish to speak to Reggie?'

'We are investigating a double murder.' Blizzard curled a lip at the familiar use of the killer's first name.

'Ah, yes the fires. I have to be honest, I am struggling to see how the incidents can be linked to Crake Lane or Reggie, though.'

'One of our suspects is an English Literature student who we believe met him during poetry recitals here.'

'They do come from the university, yes. It has proved a most valuable exercise for the patients, allowing them to widen their interests and express themselves more effectively.'

'I wouldn't have thought that Reginald Morris needed any help expressing himself,' said Blizzard.

'Chief Inspector,' replied Hayley gravely, 'I appreciate that your job is to arrest criminals, but once they are here it is our job to treat their illness. We take a more enlightened view these days, and the poetry has proved a–'

'Damn it, you're letting an arsonist hear poems about fire!' exclaimed Blizzard. 'Why don't you go the whole hog and give the bastard a box of matches?'

'I don't like your attitude.' Hayley scowled; the first time the detectives had been given a glimpse behind his urbane demeanour. He quickly regained his composure. 'It is typical, if I may say so, of many of your fellow – how can I phrase it, let's say older, shall we? – officers.'

'Are you really surprised?' said Blizzard. 'How do you think the families of his victims would feel if they knew what you are doing here?'

'I hope they would realise that we are a hospital, not a prison, Chief Inspector. Our job is to rehabilitate the patients in order that they may one day be able to live normal lives.'

'I do hope that you are not saying you would release Morris?'

'He is not the only patient here. He does not so dominate our thoughts in the way he appears to do with you.'

Colley held his breath and watched the chief inspector's eyes flash with anger. Blizzard bit his lip and said nothing; he might not like the fact, but he needed the administrator's co-operation.

'However, in answer to your question,' continued Hayley, 'Reggie is assessed regularly by a panel of psychiatric experts, and they have judged so far that he is not fit to be released.'

'Some hospitals allow residents days out, though,' said Colley. 'We heard that might happen with Reginald Morris?'

'We do, on occasion, take a small group of patients out for the day, yes, Sergeant. It is an important part of their rehabilitation, but I can assure you that they are always closely supervised.'

'That man should never be let outside these walls under any circumstances,' said Blizzard. 'I want a full list of everywhere he has been in the past year and everyone he has met from the outside.'

'I don't see how that—'

'This is a murder investigation and I expect you to co-operate fully.'

The administrator saw the anger flash again in Blizzard's eyes.

'You are assured of my co-operation, of course,' said Hayley coldly. 'And since I can see no good cause to continue this discussion further, if you would like to come with me, Reggie is waiting for you...'

'Reginald,' said Blizzard, standing up. 'His name is Reginald and you would do well to remember that.'

Chapter fifteen

It was as John Blizzard said – on those rare occasions when he agreed to talk about the events which had exerted such a hold on Hafton two decades before – some faces never fade, and some men's names can never be forgotten. Reginald Morris was one such man. As Hayley led the two detectives to the interview room, Blizzard's mind was a whirl of confusing emotions. He knew only too well that virtually every police officer who had ever met Reginald Morris had felt themselves changed by the experience. Despite himself, Blizzard tended to agree that there was something unearthly about the way in which the arsonist had insinuated his way into the thoughts of those who were unfortunate enough to encounter him at the height of his powers.

Now, twenty years on, an older and much wiser chief inspector took a deep breath and pushed his way into the room, not quite sure how Morris would look after all these years. If he expected a monster, John Blizzard was disappointed. Dressed in a red and blue checked shirt and brown corduroy trousers, Reginald Morris looked like any other innocuous little old man as he sat on an easy chair and eyed his visitors with interest.

Twenty years of incarceration had done little to change his physical appearance; he remained a wiry individual, and although the weasely face had a few more wrinkles, it was largely as Blizzard remembered it from the gloomy November day when he sat at the back of the packed crown court and watched Morris sentenced. The eyes still glinted, the same ghost of a smile played on the lips, and there was the same faint stubble on the bony chin. But something had changed: the wavy hair, greying at the time of his arrest, was now thinning and white. With a jolt, Blizzard realised that Morris was now the same age as his elderly victims when he sent them to their graves. Blizzard came to the conclusion, perhaps for the first time, that the old man's time had passed. That, as Colley had said, he was history.

David Colley, instinctively aware of the turmoil being experienced by his senior officer, remained silent, surveying Reginald Morris with fascination. He came from a younger generation of police officers who had not encountered the arsonist in person and only knew him from the flashy newspaper reports and the pulp paperback books. Colley was one of those officers who knew that his was a myth which had long since outgrown itself.

As it became clear that Morris was not aggressive towards the policeman responsible for his arrest, the tension in the room relaxed a little and the officers sat down opposite him.

'I take it you won't object if I stay?' said Hayley, preparing to take his seat.

'I can't say the idea thrills me,' said Blizzard.

'I think it would be appropriate,' said the administrator. 'Reggie needs someone to—'

'I will be alright on my own,' said Morris in his nasal voice.

'But—'

'You heard the man,' said Blizzard. He gave the administrator a disarming smile. 'A cup of tea might be nice, though. Do you think you can arrange that? No sugar in mine.'

Colley stifled a laugh and was surprised to see a smile also playing on Morris's lips. Hayley glared at the chief inspector, hesitated for a moment, thought better of arguing and stormed from the room, slamming the door behind him.

'He's a bit of fusspot,' said Morris. 'He is well meaning but there's too much theory in his head, if you ask me. Now, Chief Inspector, I think I owe you an apology.'

'Come again?' said Blizzard, thrown off guard.

'It was wrong of me to threaten your life. I did not know what I was doing. Had you not arrested me on that night, I would have continued killing. You did us all a favour...'

'You needn't try it on with me. I'm not one of your psychiatrists.'

'I am aware of that,' said Morris. 'However, time has changed me, and today is the first opportunity I have had to look you in the eye and offer you a sincere apology.'

Blizzard, uncomfortably aware that he was being outmanoeuvred, surveyed his old foe uncertainly for a moment, searching the face for the taunting style of the man he once knew. In an odd way, it would have been reassuring if he had detected it at that moment, giving him something that he could understand, something to hold onto; but to his disappointment, he found nothing. Colley watched in bemusement as Blizzard struggled to come to terms with the situation.

'However,' said Morris, 'I am sure that the purpose of your visit is nothing to do with my crimes. Mr Hayley has informed me of the death of the two old men, but I am still not sure how I can help.'

'The killer appears to have learnt much from you,' said Blizzard. 'He even taunts the police with poetry.'

'I always thought that to be a distinctly imaginative approach,' said Morris. 'I suppose I shouldn't be surprised that others have adopted it. Show me the poetry, please.'

Colley fished in his pocket and handed over the piece of paper, which Morris examined with interest.

'Raymond Marriott, if I am not mistaken,' he said.

'I believe you know his work well,' said Blizzard. 'I understand that a group of university students read some of it here.'

'It was a most gratifying experience. However, if my presumed love of Raymond Marriott's work is somehow significant to your inquiry, I must disappoint you. I find his work ugly and unappealing.'

'But a lot of it deals with fire,' said Colley, speaking for the first time.

'Ah, Sergeant, Sergeant,' replied Morris with a gentle smile. 'You, like so many before you, have such a simplistic view of me. Twenty years ago, I was indeed maddened by an illness which gave me an irrational lust for fire, but through my therapy I have learned to confront that obsession. I am cured now.'

'That remains to be seen,' said Blizzard. 'It did cross my mind that you had sent the poetry.'

'Then let me put your mind at rest. I did not. They even read the letters I send to my sister so, I very much doubt that I could get some poetry out to you, even if I wanted to.'

'There are ways. You know that. There was a young man called Andy Hemmings at the poetry recital. Do you recall him?'

'Maybe the face, but not the name.'

'He was much taken with the work of Raymond Marriott,' said Blizzard.

'There was one young man like that, yes. He read rather well, as I recall.'

'Did you talk to him afterwards?'

'I may have done,' said Morris.

'About your love of fire?'

'Those crimes were committed by a man who no longer exists. I do not speak of them.'

'I've got two bodies on my hands and every reason to believe that there'll be more,' said Blizzard. 'If you've been filling some kid's head with nonsense–'

'Threats, Chief Inspector? I fail to see what more you can do to me. Thanks to you, I shall spend the rest of my life here anyway.'

'I sincerely hope so,' said Blizzard.

The inspector stood up and walked from the room without speaking further, leaving the old man alone with a surprised Colley.

'I wish I could help,' said Morris. 'But young Hemmings hardly seemed the type to go about starting fires.'

'Aye, maybe you're right,' said Colley. He had long since come to the same conclusion.

'But then, neither did I.'

Colley looked at the smile flicker across the old man's face and felt, for the first time, the uneasiness experienced by other officers who had encountered him. Hurrying out into the corridor without a backwards glance, the sergeant caught up with Hayley and Blizzard who were deep in conversation.

'You see,' Hayley was saying earnestly. 'Reggie is a changed man.'

'It was a good performance,' said Blizzard. 'That's all.'

'It was not a performance. Can you not accept that he has finally come to terms with the enormity of what he did?'

'All I saw was a convincing act,' said Blizzard. The two men started walking and Blizzard pushed open the swing doors. 'He's learnt how to say the right things at the right time.'

'There were certainly plenty of buzz words,' said Colley.

'I think that is very harsh,' protested Hayley.

'Maybe you do,' said Blizzard. 'But what worries me is that one day he'll push all the right buttons and, next thing we know, he'll be wandering the streets, clutching his box of matches; and we won't be able to do a damned thing about it.'

The remainder of the walk to the reception area took place in silence and Blizzard did not bid the administrator farewell as he strode out of the building into the bright autumn sunshine.

'I am afraid that your Mister Blizzard lives in the past, Sergeant,' said Hayley sadly, as he watched the detective stride across the car park. 'Our understanding of mental health has undergone great changes in the past twenty years. What's more, he seems to have a great many preconceptions about Reggie. Tell me, you're a young man who has not had the time to be infected by older officers: do you think Reggie is still a danger to the public?'

'I leave those sorts of decisions to the experts.'

'Don't let your chief inspector hear you say that. He thinks he's the expert.'

'You can hardly blame him where Reginald Morris is concerned.'

'He certainly seems filled with an irrational anger,' said Hayley.

'Yes, well, pardon me for sounding thick, but Reginald Morris did threaten to kill him.'

'But am I not right in thinking that Reggie has just apologised for that?'

'You weren't in the room.' Colley looked at him suspiciously. 'How do you know what he said?'

'One of our workers discussed the matter with Reggie in therapy when we knew you were coming. We saw it as an ideal opportunity for him to confront what he did to your chief inspector.'

Colley shook his head.

'The right buttons,' he said. 'Blizzard's right – you teach them what to say and they say it.'

He brushed past the administrator and set off after his chief inspector.

Chapter sixteen

It was mid-afternoon when George Ferris left his city centre office and drove the five minutes to Rider Street. Getting out of the vehicle, he looked along the rundown terrace, glanced down at the piece of paper in his hand and frowned. He looked at the door of the house; the faded number said 87, alright. He re-read the note handed to him by his colleague earlier that day.

'Mr Francis,' murmured Ferris. '87 Rider Street. Wants to talk about house insurance.'

So intent was he on studying the note that he did not notice the two burly men emerge from the nearby alleyway and walk briskly towards him. When he did see them, it was too late and he could not react to the punch that was driven into the pit of his stomach, doubling him over and forcing the air from his lungs. Nor could he resist as they dragged him towards the alleyway.

* * *

Few words were spoken during the journey back to Abbey Road Police Station; David Colley staring wordlessly out of the window at the fields, John Blizzard driving in silence, inwardly rebuking himself for going to visit Morris. Like Colley, the chief inspector had come to the conclusion that his nagging suspicions about the old man's involvement in the murders were unfounded, and that his obsession had deflected him from more important questions. Nevertheless, he could not get Andy Hemmings out of his mind so, as late afternoon darkness fell over the city and the streetlights started to come on, Blizzard and Colley drove through the rush-hour traffic towards the student's house in Holbrook Street. The front door was opened by Edward Jones, his hand still bandaged.

'Is something wrong?' he asked on seeing their unsmiling expressions.

'We're looking for Andy,' said Blizzard.

'He's not in.'

'Did he say where he was going?'

'I am afraid not,' said Jones. 'What's all this about?'

'Can we come in?' asked Blizzard. He glanced at the twitching ground floor curtain in the neighbouring house. 'I don't really fancy discussing this on the doorstep.'

Jones stood aside and ushered them into the hallway. The stale smell of smoke still lingered.

'Les Melcham not found you anywhere else to live?' asked Blizzard. He eyed the scorch marks on the wallpaper and the tape stretched across the entrance to Bill Lowther's flat. 'Surely, this place is not habitable?'

Jones said nothing and led them into his ground floor flat. The officers shivered slightly in the damp chill.

'Sorry about the cold. I've only just got in from work.' Jones gestured to a three-bar heater in the corner. 'It'll warm up in a bit.'

'And I don't imagine that Les Melcham believes in central heating?' said Blizzard.

Jones ignored the comment.

'Would you like a cup of tea?' he asked instead.

When they nodded, he disappeared into the kitchen to re-emerge a few minutes later with a pot and three cracked mugs. Jones grimaced when he placed the tray on the table.

'Hand still bad?' asked Colley.

'Still a bit sore. Why are you here? Andy's not in trouble, is he?'

'Possibly,' said Blizzard. 'Are you sure you don't know where he is?'

'He sometimes goes to his parents in Nottingham, if he's got no classes on.'

'What do you know about him?' asked Colley, taking a sip of tea.

'Not a lot, really. Bit of a loner, is Andy. Spends a lot of time in his flat. We're not close. We nod on the stairs and that's about it.'

'Do you know where he was the night of the fire in Inkerman Street?' asked Colley. 'Sunday?'

'I don't.' Jones looked with consternation at the sergeant. 'Surely, you don't th–'

'Just answer the question, please,' said Blizzard.

'I'd been away for the weekend and came back about tennish. Went to bed, watched a bit of TV and dropped off. Didn't see Andy. Mind you, I heard the front door slam.'

'What time?' asked Blizzard.

'Early morning – threeish, something like that.'

'Someone coming in or going out?'

'Coming in, I think. I heard footsteps in the hall.'

'But you don't know if it was Andy?' asked Colley.

'I'm afraid not. You know what these places are like – people come and go all the time.'

'And on the night of the fire here, are you sure that Andy ran downstairs from his flat when you tried to rescue Bill?'

'Positive.'

'Are you sure about that?' said Colley. 'I mean, how can you be certain that he wasn't already there? There was a lot of smoke in the hallway.'

'Hang on a minute,' protested Jones. 'You are not honestly suggesting that Andy—'

'We have to consider every angle, Edward,' said Blizzard. 'Did he ever mention someone by the name of Reginald Morris?'

'What, the arsonist guy?'

'How come you know about him?' Blizzard looked at him suspiciously.

'I'm Hafton born and bred. Everyone knows about Reginald Morris. My mum used to talk about him. Besides, there was that television documentary a few weeks back.'

Blizzard nodded; the reply seemed to satisfy him.

'But Andy never mentioned him?' he asked.

'No, never. Why would he? He's been locked up at Crake Lane for the past twenty years, hasn't he? Listen, Andy may be a bit of an oddball, but there's no way he would set fire to Bill's flat.'

'Like I said,' replied Blizzard, draining his mug and standing up, 'we have to eliminate everyone from our inquiries. If you hear anything, let us know, eh? And tell Andy we're looking for him, but not why.'

'Yeah, alright,' muttered Jones. He followed them into the hallway. 'But I reckon you're wrong about him.'

'I hope so,' said Blizzard.

The detectives walked out into the fresh night air and over to the car, watched from the doorstep by a pensive Edward Jones.

'What do you think?' asked Colley as they got into the vehicle.

'I think I want Andy Hemmings found.'

'You still fancy him, then?'

'I don't know what I think, David.'

The car radio crackled into life.

'Important Message for Detective Chief Inspector Blizzard,' said the woman in the control room. 'Please go to the General Hospital and see Detective Inspector

Ramsey. He says that a friend of yours has had a nasty accident.'

'Will do,' said Blizzard. He glanced at Colley. 'What's the betting it's our Mr Ferris?'

'Look on the bright side. It might be Les Melcham.'

'I was never that blessed,' said Blizzard.

Chapter seventeen

The two officers met a grim-faced Chris Ramsey in the General Hospital's reception area. Ramsey, a slim, tall man with short-cropped brown hair, a thin face and prominent nose, took them up to the intensive care unit on the third floor. For a few moments, they peered in silence through the glass screen at the man lying wired up to a variety of machines, breathing only with the aid of a ventilator. Although the eyes were closed and the swollen face a mass of cuts and bruises, he was recognisable as George Ferris – but only just.

'He's your insurance man, isn't he?' asked Ramsey.

''Fraid so,' said Blizzard.

'You reckon Les Melcham's behind it?'

'Well, I don't think it's someone complaining about increased premiums.'

'More like critical illness cover,' said Colley bleakly. 'What are his chances, Chris?'

'The doctors are not hopeful. He's taken a fearful beating. Fractured skull, broken jaw, punctured lung and four broken ribs – oh, and they reckon he's blind in one eye.'

'How did it happen?' asked Blizzard. 'As if I didn't know?'

'According to a work colleague, he was called out to talk to a prospective new client. The caller asked for him personally. We are assuming it was a set-up. He was found in an alleyway off Rider Street.'

'And, interestingly enough, Rider Street is just round the corner from Inkerman and Holbrook,' said Colley. 'A warning to others to keep their mouths shut?'

'Possibly.' Blizzard turned away from the window; he'd seen enough. 'But I reckon they also wanted poor old Ferris silenced for good.'

'If he's spragged on Les Melcham, he might be better off dead anyway,' said Ramsey.

'I take it he hasn't said anything?'

'No. He was unconscious when he was found. Hasn't come round yet. Not sure that he will. As for a description of the attackers, usual story, I am afraid. We asked around in the area but blank faces all round.'

'Brilliant,' said the chief inspector. 'A bloke gets beaten to within an inch of his life and nobody sees anything. This city never fails to amaze me.'

'This has got to put Melcham in the frame for the fires in Holbrook and Inkerman, hasn't it?' said Colley.

'Maybe,' said Blizzard. 'Are you OK to stick with this, Chris? We've got enough on with Pembridge and Lowther.'

'Sure. Do you want me to bring Melcham in?'

'Not unless you want the chief constable to help you achieve your lifelong ambition to become a traffic warden. No, let's wait until we've got something definite. Ask around, see if you can link any of Melcham's heavies with this. It has got them stamped all over it... as has poor old Ferris's face.' Blizzard headed down the corridor. 'And I want a full-time guard on this place – we don't want anyone popping in to finish the job off.'

With that, he stalked down the corridor and pushed his way through the swing doors.

'He's not very happy with himself, is he?' said Ramsey as he watched him go.

'Actually, it's everyone else he's not happy with,' said Colley. 'Although if you ask me, it's a Reginald Morris thing.'

'How did that go?'

'It didn't.'

'Ah.'

Colley ambled off to join his boss by the drinks machine on the landing near the lifts. Blizzard was standing cradling a plastic cup of steaming tea in his hand.

'What if I'm wrong?' asked the inspector as Colley put his money into the machine.

'About what?' Colley cursed as the machine swallowed the coins without giving him his drink. 'Why is it that these bloody things never work properly?'

He put another coin in. The cup failed to drop and the drink poured out over his shoes. Blizzard allowed himself a smile at the sergeant's exasperation.

'Wrong about what?' asked Colley as he finally managed to obtain a drink the third time around.

'What if we're overcomplicating things with all this talk of Reginald Morris?' The inspector noticed that Colley had raised an eyebrow. 'OK, OK, what if *I'm* over-complicating things? What if it's actually very simple?'

'Les Melcham?'

'We always said that one day he'd take the next step. Try to join the ranks of the big boys. What if this is him making his move?' Blizzard thought of George Ferris. 'Making sure everyone knows that he can get away with whatever he wants?'

'Maybe.' Colley took a sip of tea and grimaced at the taste. 'But, as you said, it would be remarkably stupid to take out extra insurance then torch the places on successive nights. Surely, he'd know that we'd work it out pretty quickly? The earlier fires were several weeks apart. That's why no one made the connection, even though they were both his houses.'

'That's what's bugging me, David. It all fits too easily, and Les is too shrewd to make a mistake like that.'

'Unless someone is framing him, like he said. Those blokes from the nightclub he was talking about.'

'Could be.' Blizzard's mobile phone rang. He took the call. 'Sarah, what you got?'

'Not a lot,' said the detective constable. 'Andy Hemmings is still missing, I am afraid. Nottingham police say that his parents have not heard from him for three weeks and they're not expecting him home this weekend either. I've got a couple of guys watching the house in Holbrook Street in case he turns up there.'

'Keep on it,' said Blizzard and ended the call. He slipped the phone back into his jacket pocket and looked thoughtfully at Colley. 'And where do we think Andy Hemmings fits into all of this? And where the hell is he?'

'I hate to think,' said Colley grimly. 'I really hate to think...'

* * *

Lodge Park Road was deserted when the car pulled up outside The Cedars nursing home shortly after 2am. This time, the driver was relieved to see that most of the downstairs windows were in darkness and that no one was moving about in those rooms, which were still illuminated. He got out of the car, opened a rear door and removed a petrol can. Now the time was right.

Chapter eighteen

That night, John Blizzard had another nightmare. They were getting worse. High rise buildings blazed and terrified people dangled from windows, waving their arms wildly, their desperate screams for help rending the night air as they were consumed by the flames. As Blizzard barged his way recklessly through the crowds thronging the burning streets, he was vaguely aware of a shadowy figure, untouched by the flames, smoke swirling in front of its face; but before the detective could make out the features, the creature vanished and the sirens of fire engines were replaced by a shrill ringing.

'Not again,' groaned Fee as the baby started to cry in the next room.

Cursing, Blizzard noted that it was two fifteen in the morning and reached blearily for the phone.

'Blizzard,' he mumbled.

'It's Colley,' gasped the breathless sergeant. 'You'd better get down to Lodge Park Avenue. Our friend has really got it right this time.'

* * *

Thirty minutes later, John Blizzard realised with horror that his nightmare was nothing compared to the fire that tore its way through The Cedars. The alarms had gone off shortly after two o'clock, but even then, it was already too late for many of the residents as the night staff were confronted by a wall of fire rolling along one of the narrow ground floor corridors. One bedroom was already consumed by flames, but the courageous staff had managed to rouse two other elderly people and carry them out of the house. When they turned to go back inside to rescue the people upstairs, the main hallway was on fire and they were beaten back, forced to watch helplessly as the flames took hold.

The devouring fire tore up the stairs and swept along the landings of the upper floors, already choked with thick black smoke which billowed into the chill night air from bedroom windows through which, illuminated in the dancing flames, could be seen the twisted faces of terrified elderly people. The air was filled with their screams, the shattering of glass and cracking of timbers, the throbbing sound of fire engines and the distant wailing sirens as every available tender in the city was summoned.

The small car park in front of the home was a mass of flashing blue lights but, although numerous teams of firefighters trained their hoses onto the building, the large amount of water had little effect on a blaze which intensified with every passing second. Senior officers ran around, yelling orders to their firefighters, and the turntable ladder hovered at a safe distance, unable to get closer, two firefighters balancing precariously at the top, directing jets of water onto the blazing roof.

Behind the fire engines stood a fleet of ambulances, one of which had already ferried the two rescued elderly women to the General Hospital, where extra medical teams had been put on stand-by. Two of the three female night staff had also been taken to hospital, one suffering from shock, the other with burns to her hands and face.

The third woman sat in shocked silence inside another ambulance, a blanket round her shoulders, her hand held by a sympathetic policewoman.

A fresh eruption from inside the house prompted a hurried conference of senior firefighters.

'We've got to get a turntable ladder up to those top floors!' snapped fire chief Brian Anson, who had taken command of the operation.

'Too dangerous,' replied Tom Spivey.

'It's the only chance for those poor bastards inside!' exclaimed Anson. His eyes glinted in the flickering light.

'It's too risky, it only needs another explosion and the lads on the ladder are goners. They're too close as it is.'

'Well, we have to do something.' Anson shouted to one of the crews. 'Get that ladder pulled back! And get another hose on that roof! That gable end will go if we don't watch it.'

One of the firefighters held up a hand in acknowledgment, and the ladder gently swayed backwards, continuing to pour its remorseless jet onto the building but with little effect.

'So, that only leaves the front door,' said Anson grimly. 'What do you reckon?'

'Dodgy,' said Spivey. 'The hallway's well gone.'

'But it's our only chance. Are the stairs still intact?'

'We can't say for sure.'

'OK,' said Anson after thinking for a moment. 'Try to get your team in there and up onto the first floor.'

Spivey hesitated.

'If you've got a better idea…' said Anson.

Spivey shook his head.

'I haven't.' He turned to go.

'But listen, Tom,' added Anson. 'No heroics, do you hear? If it gets dodgy, get them out of there. Right?'

'What do you mean "if" it gets dodgy?'

Spivey ran off to brief his team. Moments later, four figures wearing breathing apparatus and dragging two hoses raced forwards and dived into the building, their progress covered by jets of water from fellow fire fighters. Seconds later, there was a dull roar deep within the house and a huge explosion of flames and smoke.

'What the hell was that!' cried Spivey in alarm.

Three shadowy shapes emerged from the building, one of them limping badly.

'What the hell happened?' exclaimed Spivey, rushing up to him.

'Staircase came down.' The firefighter's eyes were wide with fear.

'Where's Alex?'

'Still in there. Caught the full weight of it.'

'Shit!' breathed Spivey. He yelled at another firefighter. 'Diane, get a rescue team in there!'

She nodded and rushed off to orchestrate a fresh assault on the building.

'What's it like in there?' asked Spivey as the firefighter sat down and allowed an ambulance officer to bandage his gashed arm.

'Bad. I can't see us getting onto those upper floors now.'

'Neither can I,' said Spivey grimly. 'I'm afraid we've lost this one.'

'I don't reckon there's anyone left alive anyway. It's an inferno in there – they didn't stand a chance.'

Spivey realised that the screams of the old folk had stopped and that the only noise now was the crackling flames and the gush of water; he was also acutely aware that he had lost a firefighter under his command for the first time and felt a coldness in the pit of his stomach.

'Damn it,' he breathed.

Noticing the ashen-faced Blizzard and Colley watching in horror nearby, he walked over.

'I just hope this isn't the work of your man,' he said.

'So do I,' replied Blizzard quietly.

* * *

Within half an hour, the fire started to burn itself out and the fire crews gained the upper hand for the first time. Eventually, the final flames were doused and the first light of morning streaking the sky revealed the stark enormity of what had happened. The Cedars had been reduced to a gutted shell – timbers scorched and smouldering, roof skeletal, walls cracked and blackened. Exhausted firefighters packed away their equipment and Blizzard and Colley watched in silence as the bodies were brought out, as did the growing crowd of people gathered in the road behind police tapes.

'How many have died?' said Blizzard quietly.

'Eight,' said Colley. 'Mainly women, one old fellow – and the firefighter. There's another six injured, one member of the night staff, the rest elderly. Four of them are touch and go.'

'Hellfire.'

'I think you may be right.'

A weary Spivey came over, the thick black grime failing to hide the pain on his face.

'I'm sorry about your boy,' said Blizzard softly.

'So am I.' The strain was clear in Spivey's voice. 'There's no way this was an accident.'

'What makes you say that?'

'I've just seen the body of the old fellow in the ground floor bedroom, where we think it started. It's very similar to the others.' Spivey grasped the chief inspector's arm. 'Make sure you get the bastard that did this – I've lost a good man here tonight.'

'We will,' said Blizzard through tight lips. He turned to the sergeant. 'David, I want Andy Hemmings, and I want him now...'

Chapter nineteen

The knocking which reverberated round the quiet street was loud enough to wake the dead. John Blizzard dearly wished that it could, as he stood in the misty half-light of early morning, watching his sergeant hammering on the door to the house in Holbrook Street. After a few moments, it was opened by a bleary Edward Jones, dressed in his pyjamas and rubbing the sleep from his eyes.

'What the hell...?' he mumbled when confronted by the two stern-faced detectives.

'I want Andy Hemmings, and I want him now,' said Blizzard.

'I told you last night – he's not in. What's this...?' Blizzard pushed past him and entered the house. 'Hey, you can't do that.'

Blizzard ignored the protestations and bounded up the stairs, ignoring two bemused young women who had appeared on the landing in their nightwear.

'What on earth has happened?' asked Jones as he and the sergeant followed him.

'Someone just killed eight people – and your mate Andy is missing.'

'Jesus,' croaked Jones. He slumped against the wall halfway up the stairs. 'Another fire?'

'An old folks' home. They didn't stand a chance.'

Jones shook his head. 'No, no,' he said. 'I just can't believe that Andy would do a thing like that.'

'Well, someone did.'

There was a splintering sound from upstairs as the chief inspector kicked in the door to Hemmings' first floor flat. Colley sprinted up the stairs to find the chief inspector sitting on the bed and gazing bleakly across the room.

'I should have realised earlier,' he said as the sergeant entered the room.

'You had no evidence against Hemmings,' said Colley. 'And for all we know, he may not… Oh…'

His voice tailed off as he followed the chief inspector's gaze to the sheaf of papers lying on the student's desk. Colley did not need to look closer to see that they were handwritten poems.

'I bet if we compare the writing style to the ones I received, we will find a match,' said Blizzard. He walked across the room and opened a cupboard door. 'Let's see what else he's got that we're not supposed to see.'

The detectives stood in silence and surveyed the books lined along the shelves. Every one of them was on the subject of true crime; the exploits of the world's most evil killers chronicled in neat alphabetical order. Andy Hemmings had been assembling a library of murder. Blizzard's eyes lit on one volume, in particular, and he cradled it thoughtfully in his hand. Titled *A Flicker In The Night*, it was a particularly lurid chronicle of the criminal career of Reginald Morris. The inspector looked closer and noticed the author's name. Gary Mistry.

'So, that's why he was asking all those questions,' he said. 'To sell a few more copies.'

Switching his attention to the killer's face leering out of the front cover, Blizzard felt a familiar shiver run down his spine, and the ghosts that had been banished during the visit to Crake Lane came slinking back.

'What is it?' asked Colley.

'The legacy of Reginald Morris.' The inspector tossed the book to the sergeant. 'Written by our Mr Mistry.'

Blizzard turned to look at the ashen-faced Edward Jones, who was standing at the door.

'Did you know about this?' he asked.

'Reading isn't illegal.'

'Time to stop defending him,' said Blizzard. 'Can you explain why he has all these books?'

'Andy's fascinated with crime – he wants to be a criminologist. He's thinking of doing a post-graduate course on it when he's finished this one.'

'Why didn't you tell us earlier?'

'I didn't want to get him in trouble.'

'Tell that to the people in the city mortuary.'

'Look here,' said Colley. He snatched another, thinner volume from the shelf. 'Raymond Marriott. I reckon this is the same book that Sarah bought from the shop in Portland Street.'

The sergeant flicked through the pages.

'Yeah.' He held up the book at one of the verses. 'Here's the poem that was sent to you.'

'We have to find him before he strikes again,' said Blizzard. He looked at Edward Jones. 'Where is he?'

'I told you, I don't know.'

Ordering a guard to stand at the flat until forensics arrived, the detectives left the house. They drove back to the police station, dawn streaking the sky, with a silent and anxious Edward Jones in the back seat. Once there, Colley disappeared to take the electrician's statement, and Blizzard walked slowly along the corridor to Ronald's office.

'He's been at it again,' said the superintendent quietly. He passed the chief inspector a brown envelope.

Blizzard felt sick as he sat down and stared at his handwritten name and the word 'Personal' in capital letters.

'The bastard's toying with us,' he said. He pulled out a sheet of paper and scanned the lines.

'What does it say?'

'It says: "You never did appreciate the power of poetry, Chief Inspector. Well, you will soon come to understand what is meant by shrieking tongues of flame which send walls crashing as buildings tumble and crack. Death will come to a world that has not learnt to learn, of that you can be sure. Sleep well – if you can".' Blizzard looked at Ronald. 'When did this arrive?'

'It was posted in the city the day before yesterday, but it got mislaid in the post room. Turned up half an hour ago. Sounds like he was warning you about The Cedars, John. And before you ask, forensics say the envelope is clear of prints, just like the others.'

'He's clever, I'll give him that. Interestingly, Andy Hemmings has a number of books on forensic science. He probably knows all the tricks.'

'You sure it's him, then?'

'You should see his bookshelves.' Blizzard closed his eyes and groaned. 'And we had him in our hands.'

'Well, we need him off the streets as soon as possible. He's out of control and people are panicking. We've been inundated with calls from worried people, and social media is going crazy. You need to see this.'

Ronald turned his laptop round so that Blizzard could read the online article by Gary Mistry, on *The Daily Herald* website. Titled *Why have the police not learned the lessons from history?*, the opening line read: *Police in the northern city of Hafton are coming under increasing pressure to catch a mass murderer who appears to be mimicking the exploits of arsonist Reginald Morris from twenty years ago.*

'That's all we need,' said Blizzard. 'The man's a bloody troublemaker.'

'Be that as it may, it's what a lot of people are saying.'

The desk telephone rang.

'Ronald,' said the superintendent, taking the call. He listened for a few moments before replacing the receiver. 'That was Versace. Forensics have found a box of matches dropped on the path outside The Cedars. They're thinking it was used to start the fire. And one of the uniformed bobbies searching the grounds has found a petrol can in some bushes.'

There was a knock on the door and the press officer John Gittings walked in, dressed in his customary grey jacket, dark tie and trousers.

'I take it the press pack is clamouring at the door?' asked Ronald.

'You could say that,' said Gittings. 'And they're going to huff and puff until they blow the house down. I take it you've seen Mistry's piece?'

'We have, yes. We'll hold a press conference at ten.'

'I'd make it eight, if you can,' said Gittings. 'And be warned, you can expect a rough ride. Ten murders in a week isn't exactly the best advert for our neighbourhood watch scheme.'

* * *

At eight o'clock, Blizzard and Ronald found themselves sitting next to fire chief Anson in the briefing room at Abbey Road Police Station, facing a large number of expectant journalists. The tension in the air was almost physical. Colley leaned on a wall at the back, nodding occasionally to local journalists whom he knew. There were also a lot of faces which he did not recognise – the killings had excited the national newspapers' lust for the sensational. The sergeant noticed Mistry sitting amidst their ranks; the journalist spotted him and gave the merest of winks.

'Thank you for attending, ladies and gentlemen,' said Ronald. 'You have been given a press release with details of last night's incident. As you will be aware, one of the city's firefighters also died last night; Mr Anson will be able to answer questions about him. The police service, of course, extends its sympathies to the fire service for their sad loss. Now, does anyone have any questions?'

'Yes,' said Mistry, standing up. 'Are you now prepared to confirm that the events of the past few days vividly recall Reginald Morris's reign of terror twenty years ago?'

'There are marked similarities,' said Ronald. He was choosing his words carefully. The superintendent glanced at Blizzard whose stony face showed no emotion. 'But as you know, Reginald Morris has been locked up at Crake Lane hospital since the day he was convicted.'

'But someone could be copying him?' asked Mistry.

'That is possible – but it's only one of a number of theories, and we have to consider them all.'

'Has Reginald Morris been interviewed?'

'I am not prepared to go into operational matters.'

'So he has,' said the journalist.

'No comment.'

'Chief Inspector Blizzard,' asked another reporter. 'Twenty years ago, you were the officer who arrested Reginald Morris. Are you confident that you can arrest this killer?'

'What do you expect me to say?'

'I think what the chief inspector means,' said Ronald hurriedly, 'is that every officer in this force is dedicated to the speedy arrest of this man.'

'Is that arrest imminent?' asked a television journalist.

'I think it is fair to say that we have a definite line of inquiry.'

'Are you prepared to go into further detail?' asked another journalist as an excited buzz went round the room.

'No.'

Colley, watching the unfolding events intently, was disturbed by a tap on the shoulder, and a uniformed constable whispered something in his ear. The sergeant gestured urgently at Blizzard, who excused himself and hurried over to his sergeant, watched with interest by the journalists.

'Thanks for getting me away from the reptiles,' he said as they left the room. 'Much more of that and I'd have ended up saying something I shouldn't have. What's so important?'

'Reynolds wants us over at the General. Something interesting about one of the bodies, apparently.'

Chapter twenty

Half an hour later, Blizzard and Colley were standing in the pathology laboratory at the General Hospital, watching Peter Reynolds sew up the scorched remains of one of the victims from The Cedars.

'Which one is this?' asked Blizzard, eying the blackened corpse.

'Patrick O'Reilly. Am I right in saying that the fire brigade and your forensic officers believe the seat of the blaze to be his ground floor bedroom?'

'That's correct.'

'I thought so. Well, his burns are strikingly similar to those suffered by both Albert Pembridge and Bill Lowther.'

'But couldn't that just be because it was such a big fire?' asked Colley. 'I mean, the place all but burnt down.'

'That was my initial thought,' said the pathologist. 'I haven't done post-mortems on the others yet, but my guess is that they succumbed to smoke before their burns were inflicted. In the case of Mr O'Reilly, however, there is little doubt that he burned to death.'

'Indicating that someone specifically set fire to him,' said Blizzard.

'Exactly, and might I suggest that you get this sick human being off the streets as quickly as possible?'

'Now, why didn't I think of that?' said the inspector.

He glared at the pathologist and stalked from the examination room, slamming the door behind him.

'You know,' said Reynolds to the sergeant, 'I think he's losing his sense of humour.'

'I wonder why that is,' said Colley.

He headed for the car park, where Blizzard was standing next to the vehicle and talking earnestly into his mobile phone.

'Are you sure?' Blizzard was saying.

'I'm sure,' said Graham Ross at the other end. 'The handwriting on the poetry in Hemmings' flat does not fit the letters that were sent to you. I'm sorry, old son. Looks like another dead end.'

'Well, dead end or not, Versace, I want that university searched top to bottom to see if there are any other poems lying about. I want every piece of handwriting checked and double-checked. Get Sarah Allatt to help you. She's already over there in case Hemmings shows up.'

'Right-o.'

Blizzard ended the call.

'Bad news?' asked Colley.

'As bad as it gets. The letters can't be traced back to Andy Hemmings. Tell me, what do we know about O'Reilly?'

'Precious little. According to the manager of the home, he's a council-funded job. No private funds to speak of and no relatives that they know about. Not locally anyway. The council is checking the records but, to all intents and purposes, Patrick O'Reilly was another nobody.'

'The killer didn't think that he was a nobody,' said Blizzard. He unlocked his car and swung himself into the passenger street. 'So, until someone tells me differently, neither do I.'

* * *

The armed gang had planned their robbery professionally. The four men, all masked and carrying sawn-off shotguns, pulled onto the housing estate in a stolen Ford Transit shortly after ten and drew up at the row of shops, where they waited for a couple of minutes outside the building society. When the security van arrived, they waited for the guard to remove the cash box and made their move.

'Drop it!' shouted one of the men, brandishing the weapon at the guard.

The startled man stared at the gun for a moment and turned back towards the van. A loud blast rang out and he fell to the ground, screaming and grabbing at his leg. Leaving him writhing in agony on the pavement, the gang grabbed the cash box, fired several more shots into the air to scare the few people who had witnessed the incident, then clambered back into the van, which pulled away with a screech of tyres. Several streets away, they abandoned the vehicle on wasteland, set fire to it and got into the stolen car that they had parked there earlier that morning. Then they melted away as the air was filled with the sound of approaching sirens. The whole operation had taken less than five minutes.

* * *

Blizzard had just turned on the car's ignition when the radio crackled.

'This is Control,' said a woman's voice. 'I've just had DI Ramsey on... you'd better get down to Telfer Road, a security guard has been shot during an attack on a security van.'

'That's all we need,' groaned Blizzard.

'And it all sounds horribly familiar,' said Colley. 'Our little friends would appear to be back on the rob again.'

Blizzard did not reply but slammed the accelerator to the floor.

Chapter twenty-one

It was a chaotic scene in Telfer Road as the detectives' car picked its way through the logjam of traffic. Neither Blizzard nor Colley spoke, each acutely aware that the robbery was identical to one in a neighbouring suburb the previous week, in which a security guard had been clubbed with a baseball bat and a member of the public threatened with a shotgun. As Blizzard parked the car and the detectives started walking over to the security van, pushing their way through the gathering of excited onlookers, they were also acutely aware that the gang was using escalating levels of violence; it was only a matter of time before they killed someone. Maybe, the officers thought bleakly, they already had.

Chris Ramsey was talking to one of the forensics officers in the building society doorway when the officers arrived.

'What you got?' asked Blizzard.

'Same MO, guv. No doubt about it, this is the lot that did Cheriton, and they're professionals. All very slick.'

'How's the security guard?'

'Touch and go. Just missed the main artery, apparently. Mind, the doctors still reckon he might lose the leg. They're taking him straight into theatre.'

'The van?'

'Dumped a few streets away. They got into an Audi, which was nicked from outside some businessman's home early this morning.'

'You're going to have to stick with this,' said Blizzard. 'We've got enough on with the fires. Do you need any back-up?'

'It would be nice, but God knows who we can spare. I've already had to borrow a couple from East to cover other jobs.'

'Why don't you give Gerry a bell at Central – see if he's got anyone? Last time I talked to him, he was moaning that all he had to do was nick shoplifters. Talking of other jobs, any progress on Ferris?'

'One of the lads picked up a few whispers from one of his snouts,' said Ramsey. 'Looks like it was some of Les Melcham's boys who did him over, but the snout's not giving any names.'

'There's a surprise,' said Blizzard.

'Do you want me to bring Melcham in?'

'No, not yet.'

'Surely we have no alternative,' protested Ramsey. 'It's about time we stopped pussy-footing around the man. We should haul his ass in.'

Blizzard looked at him for a few moments; the normally calm detective inspector was flushed, his eyes flashing defiance.

'I understand how you feel,' said Blizzard. 'But when we get him, I want us to be sure.'

'But…'

'What would we say, Chris? We understand that some of his friends are unpleasant?' Blizzard scowled as his mobile rang. 'What now, for God's sake!'

He took the call.

'Sarah,' he said. 'Have you finished at the university? Because the DI could do with a hand over at Telfer Road.'

'I think you might want to pop over here first, guv. Guess who's turned up for his morning tutorial?'

* * *

Twenty minutes later, the chief inspector and Colley were walking along the tree-lined path beside the university's east wing. Sarah Allatt was standing outside the main entrance to the library.

'He's still in there?' asked Blizzard.

Allatt nodded.

'He's reading a book,' she said.

'Come on, then,' said Blizzard. 'Let's go and see what our friend is reading – as if we can't guess.'

There were only a few people in the library, and the detectives' footsteps echoed as they walked down the main aisle towards the hunched frame of the student, who sat at the far end with his head buried in the book, seemingly unaware of their presence. Blizzard moved to stand behind him.

'Andrew Hemmings,' he said quietly, 'I am arresting you on suspicion of murder. You do not have to say anything, but whatever you do say may be taken down and used in evidence against you.'

The young man turned and stared at him as if he did not understand, then nodded dumbly and stood up unsteadily. No words were spoken as Blizzard took the stumbling young man by the arm and led him past the wide-eyed students and into the misty quiet of the morning. Colley, left behind in the library, glanced at the book which Hemmings had been reading.

'*Serial Killers in the Twenty-First Century*,' he murmured. 'What's with this guy?'

He picked up the book and walked briskly from the room, heels clicking on the shiny floor, until the sound faded into the distance and the library returned to its sepulchral calm.

Chapter twenty-two

The questioning of Andy Hemmings took place in the interview room at Abbey Road and lasted all day. Well used to conducting interviews together, the chief inspector and his sergeant worked smoothly, an unsmiling Blizzard playing it tough and barking out the questions, while Colley adopted the softer approach, smiling reassuringly at the young man and trying to take him into his confidence when the senior detective was out of the room. None of it shook Andy Hemmings' assertion that they had got the wrong man, a claim he repeated when his anxious parents arrived from Nottingham that afternoon and hired local solicitor Arnold Dawlish to sit in on the sessions. As the late afternoon autumnal gloom shrouded the damp city outside, the officers kept firing questions at the student in the windowless room, the electric light burning with a harsh glow.

Each passing minute that the interview room door remained closed heightened the tension in a police station already buzzing, as word spread that, twenty years after he had arrested Reginald Morris, John Blizzard had arrested the old man's evil protégé. It was only a matter of time before the youngster confessed, the station's old hands said confidently; stronger men than he had cracked under Blizzard's withering bombardment. Their confidence was not shared by the chief inspector and, shortly after nine thirty, the weary policeman adjourned the questioning until the following morning.

Fee was reading a book in the living room, glass of wine at hand, when Blizzard arrived home.

'Hello, stranger,' she said.

Blizzard slumped into an armchair and closed his eyes.

'Yeah, sorry about that,' he said. He opened his eyes and reached over for the bottle on the side table. It was empty. 'Pisspot.'

'What else is a girl supposed to do when her man is out terrorising innocent citizens?'

'What's that supposed to mean?' Blizzard gave her a sharp look.

'It was a joke.'

'Well, it's not a funny one.'

'But I thought that this Hemmings lad was your fire-starter?' she said as she went into the kitchen and emerged with a glass and another bottle. 'Are you saying he's not?'

'I'm not sure that he is, no,' said Blizzard as she poured out the red wine. He nodded his appreciation. 'And I'm not sure that pushing him is doing anyone any good. We'll see what a night in the cells does for him.'

* * *

Andy Hemmings spent a disturbed night in his cramped cell, still dressed in the jeans and scruffy brown jumper in which he was arrested and covered only in a thin blanket to ward off the chill. He listened in terror as the normal litany of drunks were brought in, and the air was filled with the slamming of cell doors and the sound of foul-mouthed prisoners yelling and lashing out with fists and feet.

Hemmings lay awake and wide-eyed for hours, heart pounding, legs trembling, terrified that one of the drunks would be thrown in with him until, eventually, the police station fell silent. Still he was unable to sleep on the uncomfortable bed, fevered thoughts swirling round his mind, images of Blizzard's grim expression looming large before his eyes. Occasionally, the grille in the cell door would slide open and a face would peer in to check if he was alright, but such attention did not prove a reassurance because the revulsion in the police officers' faces was undisguised as they stared upon the man who they believed had committed such vicious crimes against the city's vulnerable old folk.

By the time Andy Hemmings was taken back to the interview room the next morning, he was in an increasingly distressed state. His replies to the remorseless questions became more and more confused, his voice nothing more than a mumble, his hands shaking as he battled the fatigue which assailed every aching bone in his body. Desperately he tried to focus on the policemen's words, but their voices seemed to echo from afar and reverberate around his throbbing head. Despite his deteriorating condition, he stuck resolutely to his story.

* * *

Blizzard called a halt at lunchtime and he and Colley trooped disconsolately down the corridor to Ronald's office.

'Well?' asked the superintendent hopefully as they walked in.

'I don't know how much longer we can hold him,' said Blizzard with a shake of the head. He sat down heavily and stared across the desk at his old friend. 'There's no way we've got enough to put him in court; my big fear is that if we push him any harder, he'll have a breakdown. He's on the edge as it is and his parents are demanding that we let him out before we do some real damage.'

'So, what are you saying? That he's innocent?'

'It's got to be a possibility, Arthur.'

Ronald looked at Colley, who nodded his agreement.

'He's not changed a single word of his story,' he said.

'What about alibis?'

'Keeps mentioning this girlfriend,' said Blizzard. 'But he won't name her, says he doesn't want her dragged into this. I don't believe there is a girlfriend – Edward Jones says that he never saw anyone – but that's not enough to hold him. Besides, we shouldn't lose sight of the fact that we may actually be dealing with separate incidents.'

'Meaning?'

'Well, there is plenty of evidence to point to Les Melcham's involvement in the first two fires – he had motive, easy access to the houses, and someone was worried enough to try to kill George Ferris after he spilled the beans. Maybe Melcham *did* do the more recent ones, but someone else did The Cedars.'

'But why would anyone target Patrick O'Reilly?'

'Now, that I don't know,' said Blizzard. 'But one thing we do…'

There was a knock on the door and a uniformed officer poked his head into the office.

'Sorry to interrupt but Hemmings' lawyer says that his client wants to make a statement.' He handed Blizzard a scrap of paper. 'And this just came through for you.'

Blizzard glanced at the message but said nothing, as the three detectives walked quickly to the interview room where the bowed form of Andy Hemmings was hunched over the table. As they entered, he looked up listlessly. One glance at the student's unshaven face with its haunted expression, strained eyes and trembling lips was enough for the detectives to realise that they had broken him. His lawyer, a sallow thin-faced balding middle-aged man, nodded at them gravely. Blizzard and Colley sat down at the table opposite the student and Ronald took a seat in the corner of the room.

'I gather your client wishes to make a statement, Mr Dawlish,' said Blizzard.

'He does not wish to prolong this questioning any further,' said the solicitor. 'He wishes to make a full confession.'

Ronald allowed himself a relieved smile and Colley glanced at the chief inspector, but Blizzard's features betrayed no emotion.

'OK, Andy,' said Blizzard, sitting down. 'Let's go over it one more time, shall we?'

'I did them all,' mumbled Hemmings, staring down at the desk.

'All what?'

'All the fires.'

'How?'

'With petrol,' muttered the student.

'Why?'

'I got the idea from him.'

'Who?'

'That bloke in the mental hospital,' said Hemmings.

There was a sharp intake of breath from Ronald.

'Do you mean Reginald Morris?' asked Blizzard.

'Yeah, he liked my poems.'

'How did you know who he was?' asked Blizzard. 'Was it the book about him in your flat?'

'No, I bought that afterwards.'

'So how did you know who he was?'

'Someone told me,' said Hemmings.

'Who?'

'That professor at the university, the one who set the visit to the hospital up. He said it was ironic that we were reading some of Marriott's stuff about fire to a man like Reginald Morris.'

'But why emulate Reginald Morris, Andy?' asked Blizzard softly. 'Why kill all those people?'

'Reginald said it gave you power,' blurted out the young man, tears welling up in his eyes.

'Take your time,' said Blizzard.

'I'm sorry,' snivelled the young man. 'It's like a bad dream. Like it was someone else who did it.'

'Perhaps it was.'

Ronald glanced quizzically at his chief inspector but remained silent. Colley watched his chief inspector intently, as they waited for the sobbing student to compose himself.

'So how did you choose your victims?' asked Blizzard at length.

'If I tell you, will you let me out of here?' asked Hemmings. He regarded the chief inspector through eyes that were red and swollen with tears.

'We'll find you somewhere more appropriate. Now, how did you come to choose Albert Pembridge?'

'I'd seen him wandering about. He was always drunk. Reginald said you had to pick those who couldn't fight back.'

'How did you get into the house?'

'The front door was open.'

'And the old man's flat?'

'I forced the door.'

'Then what did you do?'

'I sprinkled petrol all around. Then I went down and stood in the crowd and watched the house burn. Reginald says that's part of the game.'

'Some game,' said Blizzard. 'But why kill Bill Lowther? He was almost a friend. You lived in the same house.'

'I couldn't stop myself,' whispered Hemmings. 'I was going to do somewhere else, then I saw that Bill had left his door unlocked. He was always drunk on a Monday night, so I went in and sprinkled petrol all over the floor and set fire to it.'

'Then you went back to bed and pretended to try to rescue him?'

'Yeah, that's it.'

'And why did you do the old folks' home?'

'I don't know, really. There was a window open on the ground floor.'

'We found a petrol can in the grounds. Was that you?'

'Yeah, I dropped it.'

'Did you stay and watch The Cedars burn?'

'Yeah, I watched it burn,' said the student with a strange glint in the eye. 'I was hiding in the trees. Reginald says that's part of the fun.'

'Sick bastard,' breathed Ronald.

'Why tell us all this now?' asked Blizzard, ignoring the superintendent's comment.

'I just want to get out of here,' said the student desperately. He reached across the table and grasped the chief inspector's arm. 'Don't you see? I have to get out of here! Can't you understand that?'

'Oh, I understand.' The inspector looked at the solicitor. 'Will you give me a minute, please?'

Blizzard stood up and left the room, watched by the startled lawyer. After he had recovered from the surprise, Ronald rushed out and caught up with the chief inspector halfway down the corridor.

'Why have you come out?' exclaimed the superintendent. 'You've got him talking, for God's sake. What if he clams up when you go back in?'

'I'm not going back in,' said Blizzard as they walked along the corridor.

'But he's your man,' protested Ronald.

'No, he isn't,' said Blizzard and walked into his office. 'I don't know what he is, Arthur, but he's certainly not our man.'

'But you heard him!'

'I heard meaningless words. Look at him, for God's sake, we've been questioning him for more than twenty-four hours. He'd tell me the moon was made of green cheese if he thought it would get him out of here.'

'But...'

'But nothing,' said Blizzard. He sat down at his desk and Colley entered the room. 'David, tell him what Andy's mother said about him before we went in this morning.'

'I took her for a cup of coffee, and she let slip that he's got a history of mental illness. Nothing dramatic, visits to the school psychiatrist, that sort of thing, but it's left him a bit unstable and he doesn't handle pressure well. He's a bag of nerves at exam time, apparently. She reckons he may even be taking drugs to calm himself down.'

'But it doesn't mean that he's not our man,' said Ronald. 'And why didn't she tell us this earlier? It's very convenient, isn't it? Just when we are closing in on the truth.'

'She was frightened that it would count against him.'

'It might still do,' said Ronald. 'And it doesn't change the fact that he has admitted these crimes.'

'Haven't we learned anything from experience?' said Blizzard wearily. 'What about Donald Creggan three years ago? The lads over at East sub-division questioned him about that murder for 48 hours, at the end of which he coughed to the lot even though it should have been patently obvious to everyone that he was nowhere near the house at the time. And remember what happened then – the Appeal Court quashed the conviction and the judges slagged off Eddy Bates for oppressive questioning. Damn near ended his career. Well, I'm not about to do the same thing.'

'But how can you be sure?' asked Ronald.

'He made mistakes all the way through his confession, Arthur. For a start, the lock to Pembridge's flat was not forced. There's no way the university professor said it was ironic that they were reading poems about fire to Morris, because he had never heard of him until I told him who he was. And Hemmings is wrong about there being a window left open at The Cedars because it was one of the first things we checked, and they had them closed – ironically, it was to protect the residents from the cold. Do you want me to go on?'

'But he knew about the petrol can under the bush at The Cedars?' pointed out Ronald. 'Surely only the killer would know about that.'

'Yes, but it was me who mentioned it first, remember.' Blizzard held up the piece of paper he had been handed earlier. 'This is what came in before we went back into the interview. It says that a bloke walked into Holland Street police station and confirmed that he left the can there after his car ran out of petrol outside The Cedars and he had to walk to the nearest filling station.'

'Why did he not come forward earlier?'

'Terrified that we'd think he started the fire,' said Blizzard. 'So would you be. The filling station has confirmed his story. There's no doubt that Andy Hemmings is sick, maybe he even believes that he started those fires, but he's as innocent as you or me.'

'But he did meet Reginald Morris at the hospital.'

'I never thought I'd hear myself say this, but I think Morris was telling us the truth,' replied Blizzard. 'He's a wily old fox and knows his only chance to get released is to con the psychiatrists that he has put his crimes behind him. There's no way he would risk some student blurting out that they spent an afternoon gassing about how to set fire to old people.'

'And what are your thoughts on all of this, Sergeant?' asked Ronald morosely.

'It does sound logical,' said Colley. 'And it wouldn't be the first time that someone confessed to something they didn't do. Lenny Barratt down St Helen's Lane – you know him, the one with the funny hat and the three-legged whippet – has been doing it for years. He even confessed to killing his father and the old codger is eighty-six and still goes dancing on a Saturday night.'

'What would you say if I said I'd heard enough to justify charging Andy Hemmings?' asked Ronald.

'I'd say you were too good a policeman to make a mistake like that.'

'I suppose you're right. Flattery will get you everywhere.' Ronald sighed. 'I knew it was too good to last. So, what do we do with Hemmings?'

'I'll ask the lad's mum to let us commit him as a voluntary patient to a mental hospital...'

'Not Crake Lane, I trust,' said Ronald sardonically.

'I think not,' said Blizzard with a half-smile. 'I was rather thinking of Hallgarth House, actually.'

'But it's not secure, is it?'

'Secure enough. We'll tell them to make sure he doesn't go walkabout, and we'll have the place watched until we get this thing cleared up.'

'I don't mind telling you that all this makes me uneasy,' said Ronald. 'What if you're wrong? What if he gives us the slip and kills someone else?'

'Then that person's blood will be on my hands,' said Blizzard. 'And I will have to live with that for the rest of my life. It'll give me something to think about on point duty...'

Chapter twenty-three

Blizzard had just finished bathtime with the baby that evening and was carrying him into the bedroom, when he heard his mobile phone ringing downstairs. The inspector cursed and carried the child out onto the landing to see Fee climbing the stairs with the phone in her hand and a resigned look on her face.

'It's Chris Ramsey,' she said.

'Will it never end? Blizzard handed her the baby and took the phone. 'Chris, where's the fire? On second thoughts, let me rephrase that.'

'No fire, thank goodness. Sorry to disturb you but Control has had a call. Someone spotted a group of four men acting suspiciously on the Canvey Hill estate. Thought he saw one of them with a sawn-off. I'm wondering if there may be a link to the building society jobs.'

'Could well be.'

'I know it's a sensitive one but can we go in? Kick down a few doors?'

'Do you really need to ask?'

'I wouldn't normally, but the description matches Graham Parris and knowing his links with Les Melcham, I thought I'd better run it past you first. Melcham owns some of the flats as well, I think.'

Blizzard hesitated, but not for long.

'Go for it,' he said. 'Give me half an hour and I'll go with you. Rustle up some troops, will you? Best let the firearms guys know as well.'

'Will do.'

Blizzard slipped the phone into his pocket and went into the bedroom, where Fee was placing the baby into its cot.

'Something big?' she asked.

'Canvey Hill.'

'Ah.' She watched as he put his coat on. 'You are going to take some leave when this is over, aren't you?'

'Promise.' He leaned over to kiss her. 'Don't wait up.'

'I never do,' she said.

* * *

Less than an hour later, Blizzard was driving Ramsey towards the desolate wasteland of maisonette blocks just outside the city centre. Built in the sixties, they had long since fallen into neglect; those flats still occupied were riddled with damp, the vandalised lifts perpetually out of action, the stairwells littered with syringes and the walkways stinking of stale urine. Although Hafton Police prided themselves on not having no-go areas, Canvey Hill had come perilously close with the arrival of gangs of drug dealers who, with gun, knife and baseball bat, had declared themselves the new lawmen.

Blizzard had been seeking an opportunity to wrest back the initiative so, shortly after eight o'clock, he and a team of armed officers moved silently onto the estate, their movements cloaked by a darkness more pronounced on the Canvey Hill than anywhere else in the city, since all its streetlights had long been shot out. The armed response team edged their way slowly round the edge of the main quadrant unseen and slipped into the inky blackness of the stairwell. Followed by Blizzard, Ramsey and Colley, all wearing bullet-proof jackets, the team climbed up to the third floor where surveillance suggested that the gunman was hiding out.

'Leave it to us now,' whispered the head of the firearms team, eyes glowing white in the darkness.

'My pleasure,' said Blizzard.

It was all over very quickly. The waiting detectives heard the scuffle of running feet along the walkway, the clatter of the door being kicked down and startled shouting, followed by several loud thuds. Then silence.

'Alright, sir,' shouted the head of the firearms team.

Blizzard let out a sigh of relief and led the detectives along the walkway and into the flat, where armed officers were training their guns on four glowering men. He exchanged delighted glances with Ramsey. Two of them he didn't recognise, but the others he knew only too well – Graham Parris and Ronnie Burnett were two of Les Melcham's henchmen.

'Bingo,' said Blizzard.

He patted a triumphant Ramsey on the back – this was better than he could ever have hoped for. The arrested men glared through dull eyes as the detectives searched the sparsely furnished flat, revealing a large quantity of cash, two sawn-off shotguns, a baseball bat and several hundred pounds worth of cocaine in bags.

'Well, gentlemen,' said Blizzard, holding up some of the cash. 'Since I assume that you didn't win this on the bingo, I think we might repair to Abbey Road Police Station for a chat about this, don't you? Maybe get our Mister Melcham in for a natter as well, eh?'

There was no answer from the men, but John Blizzard didn't mind. He was already visualising the moment when he arrested Les Melcham for armed robbery. Two hours later, though, his mood was considerably darker as he and Ramsey sat in the interview room and stared across the desk into Parris's pock-marked face. Next to Parris sat the lawyer Paul D'Arcy.

'Come on, Graham,' said Blizzard. 'Quit the games. We can tie you to the guns and the guns to the armed robberies. Wouldn't it make more sense to start talking to us?'

'My client wishes to make no comment at this stage,' said D'Arcy.

'He'd be well advised to think again,' said Ramsey. 'His prints are all over one of the guns and ballistics reckon that it matches a casing recovered from the scene in Telfer Avenue. He's bang to rights.'

'He will not be saying anything,' said D'Arcy.

'Look, Graham,' said Blizzard, leaning forward, 'I am prepared to believe that you did not shoot the security guard, but I know that you were there. Whatever happens, you are going away for a long stretch so, why not help yourself and co-operate?'

'Co-operate how?'

'Everyone knows that you and Ronnie work for Les Melcham, and I think he was behind the robberies.'

'You have no evidence to support that statement,' said the lawyer. 'Mister Melcham is a respectable member of society and...'

Blizzard stood up. He'd heard enough.

Chapter twenty-four

Sarah Allatt had just made the first cup of tea of the morning and sat down at her desk in the deserted squad room when the phone rang.

'CID,' she said into the receiver. She nodded a welcome at a couple of detectives who had just walked into the room. 'DC Allatt speaking. How can I help?'

'Hello,' said a woman's voice. It had a soft Irish lilt to it. 'My name is Rosemary Ledwith. I have just had a visit from my local police telling me about Pat and saying that you wanted to speak to me.'

'We do, yes.' Allatt reached over to pick up a piece of paper that was lying on the next desk. It bore a faded photograph of Patrick O'Reilly, which had somehow survived the fire at The Cedars. 'I'm sorry for your loss.'

'Thank you, love, but we weren't close. Not latterly, anyway.'

'You are his niece, I think? Living in Portsmouth?'

'Yes, that's right; but I am not sure that I can help you. I have not seen Uncle Pat for the best part of fifteen years. The last time was a family funeral. He'd started drinking heavily by then and was very rude to people. I lost touch with him after that. Most of us did.'

'Anything you can tell us would be useful,' said Allatt. 'Was he married, for instance? Did he have children? What about friends?'

'Aunty Mae left him when the drinking got bad and he started hitting her. She died last year. They didn't have any children. As for friends…'

Twenty minutes later, Allatt replaced the receiver and looked up as a uniformed officer walked into the room. He held up a bulky package.

'Dave not in?' he asked.

'Out on inquiries.'

'Well, apparently he has been looking for these.'

He handed over the package.

'What are they?' asked Allatt.

'Employment records from Claytons Engineering.'

'Your timing could not be better,' said Allatt.

Half an hour later, she headed for Blizzard's office, clutching her pocketbook.

'I think we might be onto something, guv,' she said excitedly, walking into the room.

'If it's bad news, I don't want it,' grunted Blizzard. The continued refusal of the men arrested on the Canvey Hill estate to implicate Les Melcham had put him in a foul mood.

'I think we may have found a link between Messrs Pembridge, Lowther and O'Reilly.'

'Really?' Blizzard looked more interested and gestured to the chair. 'Well, don't just sit there grinning like the Cheshire Cat. What you got?'

'I have just found out that O'Reilly worked for Claytons Engineering for a while.'

'How do you know?'

'One of his relatives told me, and I confirmed it on the company's employment records. They've just turned up and Pembridge and O'Reilly are both there. As is Bill Lowther.'

'But I thought Lowther worked in the shipyards?'

'Yeah, that threw me at first, so I got in touch with one of the neighbours. She reckons that before he worked at the shipyards, Lowther had a job at Claytons for a few months. Not long, apparently. Just a few months.'

'Why leave so soon?' asked Blizzard.

'Made redundant – loads of blokes were losing their jobs at the time.' She glanced down at her pocketbook. 'Lowther was made redundant in 1999, and Pembridge and O'Reilly went the next year. The company itself closed the year after.'

'Interesting stuff, Sarah.' Blizzard gave her an approving look. 'Good work.'

Colley walked into the room.

'You heard this?' asked Blizzard.

'Yeah, Chris has just been telling me.' The sergeant sat down. 'What do you reckon?'

'That, so far, we've been looking for something that links Pembridge, Lowther and O'Reilly, but that the company may be the real target.'

'Someone with a grudge against a company which closed the best part of twenty years ago?' said Colley.

'Why not?'

'You do realise that means tracking down every name on that employment list, don't you?' said the sergeant. 'There's nearly three hundred of the buggers. God knows how many of them are still alive.'

'It's got to be worth a look, though, David. Let's get everything we can. The factory's been standing empty for years – I want to know if there have been any recent vandalism attacks on it, particularly fires.'

'The kids are always getting in and setting fire to the place,' said Colley. 'I used to be one of them when I was a nipper.'

'So, we add you to the list of suspects.'

There was a light knock on the door and Chris Ramsey stepped into the room.

'This a party?' he said.

'Sort of,' said Blizzard. 'What you got?'

'One of my informants has given me a name for the George Ferris attack. You won't be surprised when you hear that it's Big Pete Hooper.'

'Another of Les Melcham's muscle-men,' said Blizzard.

'Yeah, I did wonder if it was him when I heard the descriptions. Anyway, I'd like to pull him in once I've finished with the armed robbery. The CPS reckon we've got more than enough to charge them. Surely, now has got to be the time to bring in Les Melcham as well?'

'Not yet.'

'But…'

'You know what his lawyer's like, Chris. You can go ahead with Hooper but let's hold off on Melcham until we know where he fits into things. For all we know, he could yet turn out to be our prime suspect on the fires.' Blizzard noticed the disappointed expression on Ramsey's face. 'Don't worry, we'll get him. Just got to be sure. I don't want him slipping through our fingers because we got something wrong.'

Blizzard looked at Colley.

'Talking of prime suspects, David,' he said, 'how is Andy Hemmings this morning?'

'Spent a quiet night at Hallgarth House, apparently. I hope you're right about him. I mean, if he is guilty and we've let him go…'

'I know, I'll be on traffic duty before you can say 'Chief Constable'. But the place is secure, so we should be alright.'

The desk telephone rang, and the chief inspector listened for a couple of minutes, occasionally frowning and grunting his replies. Eventually, he replaced the receiver and looked bleakly at his sergeant.

'Bad news?' said Colley.

'You'd better get my big pointy hat out. Our Mister Hemmings has gone walkabout. So much for secure.'

Chapter twenty-five

As Blizzard guided his car out of the Abbey Road yard and into the busy rush hour traffic, his expression was grim and angry.

'So, how on earth did Andy get out?' asked Colley, who was in the passenger seat.

'Good question, David, and one that I will want answering. I'm not going to let this go.'

'What happened?'

'He was due to see a psychiatrist this morning, but when they told him last night, he became increasingly agitated. When they checked his room this morning, he'd had it away on his legs.'

'Did they not check on him during the night? Our lot always do.'

'They did it a couple of times, yes, but the girl who was supposed to do the 4am one got waylaid on something else, so the next check was three hours later, by which time he'd gone.' Blizzard slapped the steering wheel. 'Bloody quacks!'

Colley said nothing but thought back to his conversation with Martin Hayley at Crake Lane; there were times when the sergeant wondered about the inspector, times when his desire to solve crime overrode his more human instincts. Both Colley and Blizzard had undergone the training about mental health, but the sergeant was not sure how much his boss had taken in.

For his part, Blizzard was still angry at the blunder as he pulled into Holbrook Street. A few moments later, the detectives were in Edward Jones's damp little flat, the young man eying them suspiciously.

'I take it this is about Andy again?' he said.

'I am afraid so,' said Blizzard. 'Have you seen him?'

'No, I haven't. Why don't you leave the poor lad alone? You know he's innocent now, for God's sake!'

'What makes you say that?' asked Blizzard sharply.

'The radio said that you'd arrested someone, then let him go without being charged. I figured it had to be Andy.'

'I'll be straight with you, Edward. Yes, we did arrest Andy; yes, we released him. He's now a voluntary patient at a mental health unit.'

'Why?'

'He's an unstable young man.'

'So would you be, if you'd been arrested and falsely accused of killing all those people.'

'Point taken,' said Blizzard. 'The problem is that now he's gone missing again, and we need to find him quickly.'

'Why should I help you?' asked Jones. 'You're harassing the poor lad.'

'You should help us because I am worried that Andy could harm himself, the state he's in.'

Jones considered the comment.

'If you're trying to trick me,' he said.

'I'm not,' said Blizzard. 'I am genuinely worried about him.'

Jones nodded.

'I'll do everything I can,' he said.

'Thank you,' said Blizzard. 'Is there anywhere he might have gone?'

'Just his parents in Nottingham.'

'We've already checked,' said the sergeant. 'Andy mentioned a girlfriend; do you know where we can find her?'

'I've never seen anyone round here but, like I said, we're not really all that close. Have you asked the other students on his course?'

'We've got someone out doing that,' said Blizzard. 'Listen, if he gets in touch, will you ask him to ring me? If he is innocent, then he has nothing to fear from the police.'

'He'll take a lot of convincing.' Jones ushered them to the front door. 'But I'll do my best – if only to help Andy.'

Blizzard nodded and walked out into Holbrook Street. Once at the vehicle, he tossed the keys to the sergeant.

'Take the car back to the nick, will you?' he said.

'Where are you going?'

'I need to think. Whichever way I turn, I'm damned. If Edward Jones is right, I have pushed a vulnerable young man to breaking point. If he's wrong, I have allowed a dangerous man to go free.'

'Yes, but…'

'I'll see you back at Abbey Road.'

* * *

Head down, hands thrust deep into his trouser pockets, Blizzard walked down the street. He walked for twenty minutes, hardly aware of the people who passed him or the blaring transistors and cheerful whistling and banging of the workmen renovating some of the terraced houses. Engrossed in his own dark thoughts and repeatedly chiding himself for the error of judgement which allowed Andy Hemmings out of his custody, the chief inspector eventually arrived at the wasteland near the railway station and walked across to the preservation society shed.

Once inside, he made himself a cup of tea and sat amid the tools and wires and rusting locomotive parts. He sat there for a long time, his thoughts back in the dingy courtroom where Reginald Morris was sentenced all those years ago. He could still remember the twisted look on the evil little man's face as, while being taken down to start his sentence, the judge's condemnation still ringing in his ears, Morris had wrestled himself free of his guard. Blizzard remembered the wicked glint in his eyes and the way his knuckles glowed white as he grasped the edge of the dock and rasped at the startled young officer: 'However long it takes, I will get even with you. You will regret the day you ever met me!'

'I'm afraid that day arrived a long time ago, Reginald old son,' murmured Blizzard.

He closed his eyes as the words echoed down the years and the chief inspector smelt again his own fear.

'I guess now we're even...'

Chapter twenty-six

It was a subdued John Blizzard who sat in the superintendent's office later that morning, shifting uneasily under his old friend's stern glare.

'So, exactly how do you suggest I tell the Chief Constable that we let our prime suspect go?' asked Ronald.

'No magistrate in the land would have granted us extra time on what we had, Arthur. You know that.'

'But we had a confession, damn it!'

'And that's all we had,' said Blizzard. 'You know the law; uncorroborated confessions are not enough and there was absolutely nothing else to connect Hemmings with those fires. Can you honestly tell me that I had enough to charge him?'

'Probably not,' admitted Ronald reluctantly.

'There you are, then,' said Blizzard. He was acutely aware that it didn't sound entirely convincing. 'But you're right, I've not handled this as well as I could have done, and it's not fair that you should face the music on my behalf.'

'I've been doing that for years, old son. I'm thinking of taking up the violin so I can join in.'

An uncomfortable silence settled on the room. Even the closest of friendships can become strained at times, and both senior detectives looked up gratefully as Allatt knocked on the door and entered the office. The troubled expression on her face banished any optimistic feelings that they may have had.

'Sorry to interrupt,' she said, 'but we've found some more poems. Forensics reckon they may match the letters sent to the chief inspector. And they say that, at first glance, the writing is similar to Hemmings'. Not a perfect match, but pretty close.'

'Excellent work,' exclaimed Ronald. 'Where?'

'Hidden in the university's boiler room.'

Blizzard closed his eyes.

'Surely you can't doubt it's Hemmings now, John,' said Ronald.

'I admit, on the face of it, that does sound pretty damning,' replied Blizzard. He sighed. 'Very damning indeed.'

'So, what do I tell the Chief Constable now? And it had better be good, or else you and I will be directing traffic on the ring road.'

'Tell him bollards,' said Blizzard.

'Sometimes, John...' said Ronald. But he allowed himself the faintest twitch of the lips.

It was the last time any of them smiled during what turned out to be a long and frustrating day. Initial optimism that Andy Hemmings would be quickly recaptured evaporated as the hours dragged by. The hunt was one of the biggest police operations the city had seen; every available officer, including a team of dog handlers, scoured every street, back alley, outhouse, estate, shopping centre, industrial area and derelict piece of wasteland, while the helicopter conducted huge sweeps of the city and surrounding countryside. Local and national television and radio stations also ran the story but, despite the intensive efforts to track him down, Andy Hemmings remained frustratingly elusive; there were no sightings, no calls from the public, nothing. To all intents and purposes, Andy Hemmings had vanished and, amid fears that he might strike again as darkness fell on the anxious city, the calls started coming in to the control room from concerned residents.

It was a depressed and weary chief inspector who eventually went home that night to sit morosely in his living room, sipping whisky and staring out into the darkness.

'He'll turn up,' said Fee.

'That's what worries me,' said Blizzard.

'You coming to bed?'

'No, I'll stay up for a bit.'

Sometime after eleven, he must have dropped off to sleep in the armchair because the next thing he knew he was back in the city of his nightmares, only this time all the burning buildings looked like The Cedars. The shadowy figure was there again, standing still and silent among the dancing flames and the swirling smoke, although this time it was not the leering face of Reginald Morris which stared out at Blizzard from underneath its cloaked hood, but Andy Hemmings'. He was laughing, and his eyes glowed an odd orange. Blizzard cried out and jerked awake, realising after a few confused moments that he was still in the armchair in the dimly lit living room. He glanced at the clock, which read one thirty, and struggled to his feet with a groan.

That was when his mobile phone rang, sharp and shrill in the stillness of the night. The chief inspector froze for a moment, then picked it up.

'Blizzard,' he muttered.

'Sorry, old son,' said Colley in a flat voice.

'Where?' asked Blizzard, heart thumping, veins running ice cold.

'Lavender Gardens.'

'On my way,' said Blizzard. He replaced the receiver and murmured. 'Now there is blood on my hands.'

As he dressed hurriedly, he had the irrational conviction that Reginald Morris was lying in his room at Crake Lane, laughing at him. Shaking his head vigorously, the inspector banished the thought and half an hour later was standing amid flashing blue lights, crackling radios and a night air yet again heavily laden with the acrid stench of smoke.

Lavender Gardens was a pleasant thirties cul-de-sac, a mile from The Cedars, and most of its houses were attractive bungalows standing amid generous well-kept gardens. Number seventeen was at the far end; Blizzard surveyed the shell in silence, the extent of the damage testament to the ferocity of the blaze. The house was all but destroyed, windows blown out, whitewashed exterior walls blackened, roof tattered and gaping. Firefighters sifted through the wreckage of furniture thrown out into the garden, while others packed equipment into the tenders. Two firefighters wearing breathing apparatus walked past; Blizzard nodded at them, but they shot him odd looks and said nothing.

'They're a bit confused,' explained a voice.

Blizzard turned round to see Spivey.

'Confused?' asked the inspector.

'They saw that you let the bastard get away,' said Spivey. He gestured to the wrecked bungalow. 'Now look what he's done.'

'We let someone go, yes, but whether he was the one who did this is another matter. We didn't have enough evidence to charge him.'

'This enough for you?' asked the firefighter. He pointed at the wreckage.

'Too much.' Blizzard closed his eyes wearily.

'Morning,' said a familiar voice.

'He's out of control,' said Blizzard as Colley approached. 'So, what have we got this time?'

'Same story,' said Colley. 'Old boy falls asleep, fire starts and spreads rapidly, body badly burnt.'

'Who was he?'

'A seventy-four-year-old widower called Harold Bainbridge. He'd lived here for at least ten years.'

'He didn't live in the Inkerman Street area before that by any chance, did he?' asked Blizzard.

'Not as far as I can ascertain,' said Colley. 'And no one round here has heard of Andy Hemmings. Or Les Melcham, for that matter.'

'Not exactly his world. Is there any connection with Claytons?'

'Not sure. Sarah's on her way to the nick to check through the company records, but there is one interesting thing: before he retired, Bainbridge used to run his own engineering business. Maybe there's a link there.'

'Maybe. OK, I'd better have a look inside.'

The detectives walked up the drive between the tidy flowerbeds and into the charred bungalow, wrinkling their nose as they were assailed by the familiar acrid stench of smoke.

'No way this was an accident,' said Blizzard as they walked into the living room and surveyed the scorched walls and furniture. 'Where's the old boy?'

'Upstairs. Front bedroom. He's a bit of a mess, I'm afraid.'

'Tell me something I don't know.'

Harold Bainbridge's body lay on the bed where he had died in agony as the flames consumed him. The detectives gazed in silence at the twisted limbs and the tormented expression on his face.

'Did he smoke?' asked Blizzard.

'I'd say he positively smouldered.'

'Thank you,' protested Blizzard with a pained expression.

'Sorry,' said Colley. 'No, he didn't smoke. Gave up years ago, according to the old dear next door.'

'Alcohol?'

'The odd drop of sherry at Christmas but that's all. Quiet, clean-living type of bloke, by all accounts. Fairly reserved but friendly enough with everyone in the road. And very fit, always walked into town, went line-dancing down the Astoria every Tuesday night.'

'None of this is making any sense,' said Blizzard. 'Different places, different types of victims, there's no pattern, and yet the more I look at it, the more I'm convinced that it's not random.'

'That would mean there has to be a link between all four of them. Surely that has to be Claytons Engineering.'

'That would be my guess.'

There was a sound at the bedroom door and a young uniformed officer entered, blanched when he saw the body, then recovered his composure and nodded respectfully at the chief inspector.

'I think you'd better come this way, sir,' he said. 'It looks like someone saw him this time.'

Blizzard and Colley hurried outside to a distressed white-haired lady who stood nervously by one of the patrol cars, clutching the hand of a sympathetic policewoman.

'This is Detective Chief Inspector Blizzard, Mrs Havers,' said the young policeman. 'Tell him what you have just told me.'

'I don't know... it's just all so awful...' began the old woman tentatively. She was unable to drag her eyes from the wreckage of number seventeen.

'Just take your time, Mrs Havers,' said Colley. He placed a reassuring hand on her arm. 'You may have seen something very important. Now, what happened?'

'It was just after midnight. I had got up to go the bathroom when I heard a noise.'

'What sort of noise?'

'Someone running. I looked out of my window and I saw a funny glow in Harold's house. That's when I saw the man passing my gate...'

'What did he look like?' asked Colley.

'He looked straight at me.' Her voice tailed off. 'It was horrible.'

'Take your time,' said Blizzard.

'I couldn't see his face properly,' said the old woman. She was struggling to steady her quivering voice. 'It was dark, and I think he had a hood on or something, but I knew he was looking at me... I could feel his eyes, you see... almost as if they were shining in the darkness.'

'Shining?' exclaimed the chief inspector. He recalled the glowing eyes of the figure in his dream, then silently rebuked himself for such thoughts.

'I can't describe it really... I'm sorry...' The woman's voice tailed off again.

'That's alright, Mrs Havers, you're doing very well,' said Colley. 'What did he do then?'

'He ran off towards the main road.'

'How old do you think he was?' asked Blizzard.

'I'm not sure, he looked like he may only be a young lad. Oh, and he was carrying a can or something like that. I couldn't see much because it was dark... three of the streetlights have been out for weeks. We keep telling the council, but they never come...'

'You've already been very helpful,' said Colley.

The woman nodded. Her eyes were drawn to the bungalow again.

'Poor Harold – such a nice man,' she said.

She started to cry, and the uniformed officer led her gently back into her bungalow, watched in silence by the grim-faced detectives.

'I suppose it *could* be Hemmings,' said Colley quietly.

'Maybe,' said Blizzard. 'Or maybe not.'

'Meaning?'

'Not sure yet.'

'What do you make of the bit about his eyes shining?'

'An old woman's imagination. I hope. Listen, make sure that the old girl has a female PC with her at all times, will you? As it stands, she's the only person to have seen our man, and I'd hate him to pay a return visit.'

'Will do.'

The chief inspector headed off, then turned back and pointed to the dark streetlights.

'Oh, and ring the council first thing in the morning, will you?' he said. 'And tell them to get these bloody things fixed.'

Colley nodded. You think you know someone, he thought.

* * *

It was shortly before 2am when the police patrol car drove slowly through Nottingham city centre and pulled to a halt at the end of an alleyway in which was slumped a young man. The officer in the passenger seat got out and walked over to him.

'Come on, son,' he said. He reached down to shake the young man by the shoulder and noticed that he was clutching a half-empty beer bottle. 'I think you've probably had enough for one night, don't you?'

Chapter twenty-seven

Dawn had barely broken when John Blizzard parked his car outside the ruins of the old Claytons Engineering works. What had been a bustling place for more than a century was now silent and skeletal, its roof having long since caved in, the guttering taken over by weeds and its windows shattered by the vandals' stones. Blizzard, a long-time student of the city's industrial history, who had even contemplated writing a book on the subject when he retired, shook his head sadly.

He closed his eyes and tried to imagine the building as it had been twenty years ago. Standing there in the misty half-light, he heard the clattering machinery, the clanking vehicles, the holler of men. A memory stirred and, for the first time in years, he thought of Dennis Briley and felt a stab of guilt that he had not kept in touch with him since he retired.

A quarter of an hour later, the inspector parked his car outside a terraced house not far from the engineering works. The front door was opened by a smartly dressed old man even before the inspector had pushed his way through the front gate.

'Long time, no see,' said Briley. He beamed a welcome.

'Yeah, sorry about that,' said Blizzard. The two men shook hands warmly. 'You know how it is.'

'I do.' Briley ushered him into the hallway. 'I wondered if you might come and see me. I was going to ring you today, in fact. I would have done it earlier, but I've been staying with my sister in Cornwall. Only heard about what happened when I got back.'

Briley gestured for Blizzard to go into the living room.

'Got quite a shock when I heard the names on the radio news,' he said.

'Well, you can add Harold Bainbridge to your list now.'

'The fire last night?'

'That's the one,' said Blizzard. 'And I suspect that you might know why they are being killed.'

Briley nodded.

'I think I do.' He walked over to a side table, opened a drawer and produced a black desk diary, which he handed to Blizzard. 'And I suspect that you'll be needing this to prove it.'

* * *

When Colley arrived at Abbey Road Police Station later that morning, having grabbed several hours' sleep, he was surprised to find the chief inspector in a remarkably cheerful mood as he sat in his office, sipping a steaming mug of tea, his feet up on the desk. As the sergeant entered, Blizzard beamed affably and gestured for him to sit down.

'David, my boy,' he said. 'How nice to see you.'

'I shouldn't let Ronald see you in this mood,' said the sergeant. He took a seat. 'I just bumped into him in the corridor and you could fry eggs on his forehead. The media have been going crackers about the fire, and the Super was in with the Chief Constable first thing. Apparently, the Chief went bonkers about Andy Hemmings.'

'The Chief Constable was bonkers to begin with. I keep telling you that. And since you ask, I am cheerful because things are going very well.'

'In case it had escaped your notice, we've got a pile of people in the mortuary, no leads of any note, Gary Mistry writing another piece saying that we have lost control, a Chief Constable who's about to explode because we left Public Enemy One go walkabout and–'

'We didn't let Public Enemy Number One go walkabout,' said Blizzard. 'Andy Hemmings didn't start any of those fires. Certainly not the one last night, at any rate.'

'Well, pardon me for being thick but, as far as I can see, we get the guy in for questioning, he coughs to the lot, we let him go and, surprise, surprise, someone else gets bumped off. Now, that all sounds pretty damning to me.'

'It certainly would be damning, were it not for the fact that at the time Harold Bainbridge was killed, Andy Hemmings was sleeping off a hefty boozing session in a police cell a hundred miles away.'

'He was what?'

'Yup. I've just had the DCI on from Nottingham. Old mate of mine, another railway enthusiast, actually. He was across here for the 25th anniversary of the Marklesea Heritage Railway last year. He reckons the 645 we were thinking of getting...'

'Skip the Thomas The Tank Engine routine. What did he say?'

'You have no soul, David. Anyway, he said that two police officers on routine patrol arrested Hemmings for being drunk in the early hours.'

'So, there's no way on earth that he could have been here.'

'Precisely,' said Blizzard. 'And that means that whoever our Mrs Havers saw last night certainly wasn't Andy Hemmings – it also means that whoever it was is still out there.'

'So how come Andy was in Nottingham?'

'Hitched a lift on a lorry at the Westbourne Road roundabout and was well out of the city by the time we got our arses into gear. The lorry driver dropped him off in Nottingham where Hemmings originally planned to go home, then changed his mind and went drinking in the city centre instead. By the time he was arrested, he was in a terrible state. It was only this morning that they realised who they had got on their hands. He's being driven back now. One thing's for sure, he's not our man.'

'But what about the handwritten poetry at the university?'

'It would be easy enough for someone to plant it in the boiler room,' said Blizzard. 'Maybe we were supposed to find it, maybe the killer only meant to cast suspicion on English students in general and got lucky with Hemmings. After all, we did rather jump to conclusions about him, didn't we?'

'Point taken. But we're still no nearer to finding our killer, are we?'

'Actually, that's not entirely true,' said Blizzard. He shot the sergeant a self-satisfied look.

'Jesus, don't tell me you ruled out our prime suspect and nabbed the real killer all before breakfast?'

'Not quite, but Sarah has been checking the Claytons employment records and it turns out that Harold Bainbridge worked there before he set up his own business.'

'You think something happened at the works twenty years ago?'

'I know so. In fact, I'd been considering the idea for a while when Sarah turned up this.' Blizzard handed over a yellowed newspaper cutting. 'I was working over on the East-side at the time, so I didn't know anything about it.'

'Interesting,' said the sergeant after reading the article. 'Very interesting.'

'It is. However, I suspect that its real significance lies in what it doesn't say. I had hoped that our own files would be more helpful but no such luck, so I went to see Dennis Briley.'

'Who?'

'Before your time, I suspect. He was a sergeant and his patch included Claytons. Knew everything that happened in that area. See, I remembered that he was obsessed with keeping a diary. Luckily for us, he hung onto them. His cupboards are stacked with them. Can't help feeling he should have got rid of them when he left the force but, thankfully for us, he didn't.' With a knowing smile, Blizzard handed over a black book. 'Read the entry I've marked with the Post-It Note.'

'Jesus, they're all here,' said Colley as he scanned Briley's scrawl. 'Pembridge, Lowther... hey, this guy, Sydney Hendrick, I've been trying to track him down.'

'Why?'

'One of the lads mentioned him when he heard I was looking for ex-Claytons blokes. I was going to go and see him today.'

'I think we both should go and see him,' said Blizzard. 'Because, if I'm right, your Mr Hendrick is the next victim.'

'It would seem so.' Colley stood up. 'We need to get to him fast.'

'He'll be safe enough until it gets dark. That's when our man strikes.'

'I suppose you're right.' The sergeant sat down again. 'I'll see if I can track down anything more on the inquest. So, what do we do about Andy Hemmings now that we know he's innocent?'

'I want him kept off the street for now. I want the killer to think we're still looking for him. I've already ordered a news blackout on the fact that we've got him again, so don't go blabbing it round the station.'

'Give me some credit,' said Colley.

'Sorry. An unnecessary remark. I apologise.'

'Accepted,' said the sergeant. He looked at his chief inspector curiously. 'Do you know who the killer is?'

'Not a name, not yet anyway, but we're getting closer, I can feel it in my bones, David. And that newspaper cutting has given me an idea.'

The desk telephone rang, Blizzard lifted the receiver and listened intently before replacing the phone and closing his eyes.

'Trouble?' asked Colley.

'I am afraid so. That was Chris Ramsey. Our friend Mr Ferris died ten minutes ago...'

Chapter twenty-eight

The acute distress tearing apart George Ferris's widow was clear to see when Blizzard and Ramsey called at the family's semi-detached house not long after her husband died. Rachel Ferris, a petite mousy woman in her mid-forties, sat on the sofa in the tidy living room, struggling to hold back the tears. Her sister, sitting next to her, was clutching her hand.

'I promised myself that I wouldn't cry,' whispered Rachel in a trembling voice.

'I know this is a difficult time for you,' said Blizzard. 'And that you answered a lot of questions at the time of the attack, but there are one or two things I must know. I understand you've had a break-in?'

'We only discovered it when we got back from the hospital this morning,' said the sister.

'He had just died,' said Rachel. She looked at the detectives through red, swollen eyes and her voice tailed off as tears welled once more.

'Take your time,' said Ramsey.

'It was me who discovered the break-in,' said the sister. 'The kitchen window had been smashed.'

'Was the house empty at the time?'

'For the first time since the attack, yes. My brother and his family have been staying here, but they went back yesterday and myself and Rachel were at the hospital when it happened.'

'They must have been watching the house for some time,' said Ramsey.

'It looks that way,' said Blizzard. He turned to the sister. 'Tell me, have you noticed anything unusual over the last few days?'

'There was something a couple of nights ago. We had just come back from the hospital when there was noise at the back and the security light went on. I looked but there was no one there. I didn't think anything of it. I just thought it was a cat. They often set the light off.'

'I gather the burglar alarm didn't go off this morning?' said Blizzard. He looked at Ramsey.

'It appears to have been deactivated,' said the detective inspector. 'And they knew what they wanted – they only went for the bureau in Mr Ferris's study.'

'Was anything taken?' asked Blizzard. He looked at the widow, who had regained control over the tears.

'I don't really know,' she said. 'He kept his work papers in there.'

'I know,' said Blizzard, without thinking of the insensitivity of what he was saying. 'We checked them through.'

'That was why he was killed!' exclaimed the widow, surprising them with a venom born out of grief. 'If you hadn't come to see him, he would have been alive today!'

'No one is more sorry than me about his death,' replied Blizzard. He tried to appear sympathetic. 'But you must understand that we are investigating a number of serious crimes and–'

'He was a good man!' Rachel Ferris grabbed hold of the chief inspector's arm. 'There is no way he would have been involved in those fires!'

'They were only doing their job, Rachel,' said the sister. 'And we can't hide from the fact that George was mixed up with some funny people.'

Rachel looked as if she were about to reply, then nodded dumbly and buried her face in a handkerchief.

'I know this is difficult for you,' said Blizzard. He shot the sister a grateful glance. 'Can I just ask if the family knew about George's debts?'

'He always liked the online poker,' said Rachel. 'But we never thought that he would be stupid enough to go to a money lender.'

'Did you ever meet Les Melcham?'

'No, but if I do, I'll kill him!'

'May I suggest that you do not go looking for him. He's a nasty piece of work.'

'Do you think he had George killed?' asked the sister.

'It's a line of enquiry, certainly. But I must warn you, Les Melcham is a clever man and, without evidence, we cannot charge him. There's a lot more work to be done before we reach that stage.'

'We'll do everything we can to secure a conviction, believe me,' said Ramsey.

'Meanwhile,' said Blizzard, standing up, 'thank you for your time. May I offer you our deepest condolences. Would you like a policewoman to stay with you?'

'No, I'll be alright. I've got Maureen.'

Blizzard nodded and the detectives left the house.

'What do you think about the break-in?' asked Ramsey as they walked down the drive towards the car.

'It's got to be the work of Melcham's boys,' replied Blizzard. 'Les must have reckoned that Ferris had something that would link him to the first two fires. And now with Ferris dead, we may be able to prove conspiracy to murder.'

'Excellent. So, what next? Are we still holding off on arresting Melcham?'

'Yes, but not for long. I want to turn the pressure up on him first. I want every one of his associates hauled in, Chris. Let's give them a real grilling. Who knows, if we put the wind up them, they might land Melcham in it?'

'Now you're talking!' exclaimed Ramsey.

As Blizzard got into his car, his mobile phone rang. It was Colley.

'David,' said the inspector. 'What you got?'

'You may wish to pop back to Abbey Road asap. Andy Pandy's coming out to play – I thought you might like to be Looby Loo. Thought I'd pick a reference that an older father might get.'

'There's nothing like a good sense of humour,' replied Blizzard. 'And take it from me, David, yours is nothing like a good sense of humour.'

'You love it, really,' said the sergeant.

Chapter twenty-nine

'It all checks out,' said Colley. He looked up from his desk as Blizzard walked into the squad room and handed over another newspaper cutting. 'Well, a lot of it does anyway. Only Hendrick and Lowther gave evidence at the inquest, but I did some checking on what your mate told you and he's right, the others were suspected as well.'

'But no one was charged?' asked Blizzard. He took a seat by the window and read through the cutting.

'No. Looks like they all stuck to the same story.'

'Not surprising,' said Blizzard. He stood up. 'Come on, time to tell young Andrew the good news.'

Andy Hemmings presented a pathetic picture as he sat next to his sallow-faced lawyer in the same interview room where he had been questioned for so long. As he hunched over the table, he was watched by Ronald, Blizzard and Colley, as well as his concerned parents. His father was a balding man of meek appearance, wearing horn-rimmed spectacles and an ill-fitting brown suit; his mother a prim little woman dressed smartly in matching black skirt and jacket. They viewed their son with deep consternation.

Still hungover from the night before, with a nauseous stomach and a throbbing head, Hemmings was a sorry sight – hair lank and dirty, hollow eyes bloodshot and haunted, chin unshaven, teeth yellowed, lips dry and cracked. The jeans and blue jumper that staff at Hallgarth House had provided before his bid for freedom were stained brown with the dirt of the damp alleyway in which the arresting officers had found him.

'You've caused us a lot of trouble, Andy,' said the chief inspector. 'Don't you think it's time to stop running and tell us the truth?'

There was an indistinct moan from the cowed student.

'I must protest at the way this whole affair has been handled,' said the lawyer.

'There's a surprise,' said Blizzard.

'I demand to know if my client has been formally re-arrested in connection with the murders about which he was questioned.'

'No, he has not – but he can be, if it makes things any easier. Now, may I proceed?'

Dawlish nodded a slight assent.

'Thank you,' said Blizzard. 'Now, Andy, let's get one thing straight – I know that you should not be here. We have got things badly wrong and we owe you an apology. *I* owe you an apology.'

There was a shocked silence in the heavy atmosphere of the interview room, until the student lifted his haunted face to stare at the chief inspector. His parents gaped at the policeman in equal amazement and even the lawyer seemed lost for words.

'Perhaps you would like to elucidate, Chief Inspector,' said Dawlish after recovering from his surprise.

'Particularly since you have pursued my boy mercilessly,' said the father angrily. 'And from what I can see, you have done nothing to stop him being named on Facebook. Or in the newspapers. It's a disgrace.'

'We have never released his name. The media found that out themselves.'

'Nevertheless, you have an awful lot to answer for.'

'I accept that,' said Blizzard. 'However, you forget that there was ample reason to suspect your son, Mr Hemmings. After all, he did confess to all the crimes of which he had been suspected.'

'You put my client through sheer torment in order to elicit that confession,' said Dawlish. 'Your actions have been nothing short of scandalous, and I shall be making an official complaint to the Chief Constable over your handling of this investigation!'

'Not another one,' murmured Ronald beneath his breath.

'You seem to forget, Mr Dawlish,' said Blizzard, there was an edge to his voice now, 'that you and your client were alone in the interview room when he agreed to give his confession. In fact, we had already taken the decision to release him. Perhaps you ought to consider that before making such sweeping comments.'

'I resent the imputation behind that remark!' retorted the lawyer. 'As far as I am concerned–'

'Perhaps you had better let the chief inspector finish,' said the student's father. He silenced the irate solicitor with an icy glare.

'But I–'

'That's enough!' rapped the father. His sharpness surprised the detectives as he took command of the situation in a manner that was in contrast to his mild, bookish appearance.

For a few moments there was tense silence but, on seeing the glint of determination in the father's expression, the lawyer gave a grudging nod.

'As you wish,' he said.

'Thank you, Mr Hemmings,' replied Blizzard. He looked at him with a growing respect. 'Emotions have already been running high enough in this city over these murders; level heads are needed to resolve the matter satisfactorily before it gets completely out of hand, I would suggest.'

'I agree,' said the father. 'Look, I can understand your initial suspicions about my son but what I can't understand is why he saw fit to tell Mr Dawlish that he wanted to admit to crimes he clearly could not have committed.'

'It's a common phenomenon, I am afraid,' said Blizzard. 'It's difficult for us to appreciate the effect of sitting in a small room having questions fired at you hour after hour. Isn't that right, Andy?'

'I just wanted to get out, so I told you what you wanted to hear,' mumbled the student. 'You had already made up your minds that I was guilty, anyway.'

'Well, some of us had,' said Blizzard. He shot a pointed look at Ronald.

'And Mr Dawlish said it would count in my favour in court if I pleaded guilty,' continued the student. 'He said we could claim diminished responsibility and get me sent to a mental hospital rather than prison.'

'A ploy which Reginald Morris used very successfully,' said Blizzard.

'I am beginning to regret the day we ever hired you, Dawlish,' said the father. He glared at the lawyer, then looked back at Blizzard. 'So, is Andy free to go now?'

'Technically, yes.'

'Technically?'

'Yes, but first, I have a proposition to put to you.'

'What kind of proposition?' asked Mr Hemmings.

'The people in this room may know that your son is innocent, but there are a lot of people out there convinced that he's guilty...'

'Thanks largely to the publicity your actions engendered,' said the father.

'Whatever you think of our actions, it does not change the fact that there is someone else out there who is convinced that we hold your son responsible for these crimes – namely, the real killer.'

'Go on.'

'It is my belief that in order to catch the killer off-guard, I need to persuade him that we have re-arrested Andy. We don't need to name him, it will be enough to say that someone is in custody. The killer will work it out. However, I can only do that if he is not released.'

'So, what would happen to him?' asked the father.

'I propose that we keep him at this police station for at least the next 24 hours. There is a comfortable suite here, which would be ideal for the purpose. In addition, your son desperately needs expert medical help, Mr Hemmings, and I would undertake to see that he receives it. It would give everyone time to decide how we approach his future treatment.'

'And give you time to catch the killer.'

'One would sincerely hope so.'

'This is all highly irregular,' interrupted the lawyer.

'He's right, John,' said Ronald. 'The boy is not under arrest.'

'And what if he refuses?' said Dawlish. 'Decides to walk out of—'

'If I got really nasty about it, I could get him committed to Crake Lane and make sure they threw away the key,' said Blizzard.

'But you don't have anything on him,' protested the lawyer.

'Believe me, I'd have no trouble justifying it. I could even throw in for good measure the fact that Reginald Morris filled his head with details about how he killed people.'

'But he didn't,' said Hemmings. 'I made that bit up to make it sound good.'

'So, the old bugger was telling the truth, after all?' murmured Blizzard. 'Maybe he owed me at least that.'

'I think you're bluffing,' said the lawyer.

'In all the times you and I have crossed swords, how many times have you known me to bluff, Mr Dawlish?'

The lawyer recalled bruising encounters with the detective and nodded.

'It seems that my client has few options,' he said.

'I don't honestly believe you would be that unfair to my son,' said the father. He looked at his wife, who nodded. 'You seem to have his best interests at heart, so we are prepared to trust you. But let us down–'

'I won't let you down, Mr Hemmings. You have my word on that. Now, if you wait here a moment, I will ensure that the suite is made ready.'

Colley, who was walking behind him as they left the room, heard the heartfelt sigh of relief as the chief inspector leant against the corridor wall and wiped the beads of sweat from his brow with a handkerchief.

'Well played,' said the sergeant. 'Well played, indeed.'

Chapter thirty

'I just hope you know what you are doing,' said Ronald.

'Now, where have I heard that before?' said Blizzard. 'Really fills a man with confidence, that does.'

They were sitting in the superintendent's office that afternoon, sipping from mugs of tea and reading the front page of the local evening newspaper's website, out of which loomed a headline revealing that police had made an arrest in connection with the fires.

'But I do know what I'm doing,' replied Blizzard. The inspector tried to look relaxed, like he believed what he was saying. Inside, there were still nagging doubts and both men knew it.

'We can't hold Andy Hemmings for ever, you know?'

'We don't need forever, Arthur. If I'm right, twenty-four hours should be more than enough to catch our man.'

'I still don't like it, John. You still don't know who he is.'

'Ah, but I know why he's doing it and that's almost as good. And now he knows that we have Andy back in custody, he will be more confident than ever.'

'That's what worries me. Are you sure it will be tonight?'

'As sure as I can be. There is clearly some kind of urgency about this. Like he wants to finish the job quickly. All we need is for our Mr Hendrick to co-operate...'

'He's back!' said Colley, putting his head round the door.

'Where's he been?'

'In town. Stopped off at the reference library to read the newspapers, apparently, then took himself out for lunch, but he's at the cottage now. According to our guys, he tried to look surprised when they approached him, but they reckon he knew why they were there. They are staying with him until you arrive.'

'Excellent,' said Blizzard. He drained his mug of tea and stood up. 'Game on.'

'Oh, and the DI says that Big Pete Hooper and a couple of his heavies have been spotted over on the East-side. Looks like they are doing their rounds. Chris is rustling up some troops and their duty inspector is OK for us to go over there.'

'They'd better be careful,' said Ronald. 'They're handy with their fists are Hooper and his mates.'

'Don't worry,' said Colley mysteriously. 'I've sorted out a little surprise for them.'

Blizzard raised an eyebrow, but Colley did not elaborate.

'OK,' said Blizzard. He headed for the door. 'We'll let Chris get on with it. You and I can go and see Hendrick.'

'Actually, I was rather hoping that you might let me play nice with Hooper,' said Colley. 'I'd hate to miss the fun.'

'Fun?' said Blizzard.

'Oh, yeah.' Colley tapped the side of his nose conspiratorially.

Blizzard looked at the sergeant's hopeful expression.

'Go on then,' he said. 'But I don't want you coming back and dripping blood on the carpet.'

* * *

It was just after 3pm when Big Pete Hooper left the back-street gymnasium on the east side of the city, in the company of two fellow shaven-head heavies in sunglasses and black polo neck sweaters. It had not been a social visit; Hooper, squat-faced and evil of eye, was Les Melcham's most trusted lieutenant and his trip to the gym had been about collecting the week's protection money from the frightened owner.

Chris Ramsey, wary of Hooper's reputation for violence, had planned his operation well. It was as Hooper stepped out into the street that he was confronted by three of the burliest detectives that Ramsey could find, their names suggested by Colley who had played rugby against them and still carried the scars. Colley himself stood next to them, relishing the encounter.

Ramsey stepped out from behind the officers and flashed his warrant card.

'Pete Hooper,' he said. 'You are under arrest on suspicion of the murder of George Ferris.'

For a few moments, it looked as if Hooper would resist, but a glance at the officers and the appearance of two police cars slowly edging their way along the road behind Ramsey made up his mind for him. He nodded his silent assent and meekly held out his hands to be cuffed. One of his gorillas looked at the powerfully built detectives, quickly agreed with his boss and held out his hands.

'Spoilsports,' murmured Colley.

The third man did not share the others' compliance, turned and started to run down the street.

'That's more like it!' exclaimed the sergeant.

The fleeing man was no match for the fleet-of-foot Colley, and the sergeant caught him within a few strides and sent him crashing to the ground with a flying rugby tackle, badly winding him. By the time the gorilla had regained his capacity to breathe, he had been cuffed, dragged to his feet and guided towards his colleagues.

'I enjoyed that,' Colley said, beaming.

'Wingers,' replied one of the rugby players. 'Always the glory boys.'

'And don't you forget it,' said Colley.

Ramsey, meanwhile, had walked up to Hooper and applied the cuffs.

'You'll not get anything to stick, you know,' said Hooper. 'You can try as hard as you want.'

'My mother always said that God loves a trier,' said Ramsey. 'Who knows, you might even find yourself tempted to give us Les Melcham?'

'Dream on,' said Hooper.

Ramsey shrugged and looked at the police van that had just pulled into the street.

'Taxi for Mr Hooper,' he said. 'One way. I suspect that he'll not be coming back.'

* * *

Blizzard was just preparing to leave his office when Sarah Allatt walked in, her eyes bright with excitement.

'He's still alive,' she said. She held up her notebook.

Blizzard stared at her in amazement.

'What, after all he's been through?' he said.

'Yes, he's in a nursing home but he's not got long to live, according to the staff. Some kind of infection. A matter of days, they reckon, maybe even hours.'

'Can we see him?'

'Not sure it'll be of much use, guv. He's been drifting in and out of consciousness for a couple of weeks. The staff reckon that his death would be a blessing.'

'A blessing and a strong motive for murder,' said Blizzard. 'Get it done so that he knows before he dies. Has he had any visitors?'

Allatt nodded.

'But you're not going to believe who it was,' she said.

The constable opened her notebook and held it up so that Blizzard could read the name scrawled there.

'What do you think of that?' she asked.

'Who would have thought it?' said Blizzard. 'Hidden in plain sight.'

The inspector unhooked his jacket from the back of the chair.

'Come on,' he said. 'Let's see if Sydney Hendrick wants us to save his life.'

Chapter thirty-one

A more unlikely central character in a murder investigation would be harder to imagine, thought Blizzard as he and Sarah Allatt sat in Sydney Hendrick's cramped living room, amid a clutter of antique furniture, sipping tea from best china cups. A faint musty smell pervaded their nostrils, not unpleasant, more like a mixture of cocoa and crumbling wood.

Hendrick's cottage was in the picturesque village of Erinthorpe, five miles north of the city, nestled amid farmers' fields, flat and bare in the wan autumn afternoon sunlight. A widower, he filled his life with reading, crosswords and classical music, characteristics which had made him unusual among his ex-workmates at Claytons. They had called him The Professor. Despite arthritis and angina, the eyes that shone out of his wrinkled face as he surveyed the officers were testament to a mind which remained sharp, undimmed by age. It was a memory which the detectives hoped would unlock the dark secrets of Claytons Engineering.

Hendrick noticed Blizzard's gaze straying to the crammed bookcase.

'I keep meaning to throw some of the books out,' he said. 'But a lot of them were here when I inherited the cottage from my mother, and I can't quite bring myself to do it. Seems somehow sacrilegious. Now, how can I help the local constabulary? I can't have picked up a speeding ticket in my old jalopy, surely?'

'I think you know the answer to that question,' said Blizzard. 'We are investigating the murder of four elderly men.'

'Yes, I read about them in the paper. A nasty business but, surely, that can have nothing to do with me?'

'I think it has everything to do with you.'

'What a terrible—'

'You can drop the act,' said Blizzard. 'I think you knew them all. I think you, Albert Pembridge, Bill Lowther, Patrick O'Reilly and Harold Bainbridge have something in common. Something that cost the others their lives. What's more, I think you have been expecting a visit from the person who killed them.'

'Why on earth would you think that?' said the old man. However, he was clearly rattled, the unease clear in his bright blue eyes. 'You are very much mistaken if you believe—'

'Because I think the killer knows about the fire.'

'What fire?'

'For God's sake, this is a question of life and death – your death, to be precise! Stop pretending that you do not know about the fire at Claytons twenty years ago and what happened to the security guard. James Marshall, wasn't it?'

The fight seemed to go out of the old man, and he slumped back in his chair and closed his eyes, his breathing shallow.

'You know about that?' he whispered.

'We know, yes. Unfortunately, we did not find out in time to save the others, but we can protect you.'

Hendrick had gone pale.

'Do you need a glass of water, sir?' asked Allatt, moving over to him.

'No, no,' murmured the old man. He regained his composure and looked at them out of hooded eyes. 'There is not a day I do not think of what happened, not a night I do not see the flames in my dreams.'

'Welcome to my world,' said Blizzard. 'Perhaps you had better tell us what happened then. Fill in the gaps.'

Hendrick nodded. For a moment or two, the only sound was the ticking of the clocks in the heavy air as he gathered his thoughts.

'We had been drinking,' he said softly. 'We knew it was against the rules to have alcohol in the workshop, but we were working late and there was no one else around except the security guard, and he wouldn't have told anyone. Perhaps we got careless; anyway, a spark from one of the machines must have ignited an oily rag or something. No one noticed it at the time, but it must have smouldered and after we left for the night, the whole thing went up and James was badly burnt as he tried to put it out. The inquest said that although we had been careless, we could not be held directly responsible for what happened.'

'A well-rehearsed story,' said Blizzard. 'One you told at the time, I think. Clearly, you are determined to lie right up to the end.'

'It's the truth!'

'It is not! It's the story you told to the inquest, but it is not the truth. Tell us how you left the poor bastard to burn to death.'

'I don't know what you mean,' said Hendrick. 'James Marshall discovered the fire after we left for the night. He was injured trying to fight it. The inquest agreed that was what happened.'

'But the coroner was not told the truth, was he? Nor were the police. The five of you got your heads together and told the same story. I'm not stupid – and neither is Dennis Briley.'

The old man started, and all the confidence and composure seemed to drain away from him. His face seemed darker and more lined, the eyes haunted.

'I thought he was dead,' he breathed. 'Bill told me that Dennis Briley was dead.'

'Well, he's not, and he still remembers you. He remembers all of you and what you did.'

'He never did believe us,' said Hendrick. 'Told us he knew we were lying but he couldn't prove it. And he was right, we stuck to our story and there was nothing he could do about it.'

'Perhaps you had better start your story again then. And tell it right, this time.'

Hendrick nodded and his face assumed a far-off expression as his mind was transported back to a chilly and bleak winter evening, to a darkened engineering factory where five men toiled in the workshop, sipping from cans of strong lager as they worked.

The workshop was dimly lit when, their work finished, the men sat at the workbench with their cans of lager and a pack of cards.

'Put another light on, will you?' said Albert Pembridge, looking at Harold Bainbridge. 'I can't see a fucking thing.'

'The bulb's gone,' said Bainbridge.

'Then light a candle.'

Bainbridge hesitated.

'It's dangerous,' he said. 'A spark in here with all this grease and...'

'Don't be such a fairy.'

'He's right, Albert,' said Sydney Hendrick. 'It's too...'

'For fuck's sake, just do as Albie says,' said Bill Lowther. His voice slurred slightly.

Bainbridge nodded; everyone knew what Bill Lowther was like when he was in his cups. He sighed, lit the candle and the men settled down to play again. After half an hour, Hendrick glanced up at the wall clock.

'Marshall will be on his rounds,' he said. 'Perhaps we should pack up and…'

'He'll not say owt,' replied Pembridge.

'He's a stickler for the rules is James,' said Hendrick.

Pembridge held up a bunched fist.

'I told you,' he said. 'James Marshall will keep his trap shut.'

Lowther grinned at the gesture.

'Yeah,' he said, 'we'll make sure he says nothing. Stop fussing, man.'

For a few moments, it looked as if Hendrick was going to challenge them, but a look at the wicked glint in their eyes made him change his mind. Twenty minutes later, they heard the sound of footsteps in the corridor.

'Marshall,' said Patrick O'Reilly. He looked at Hendrick. 'Maybe you had better put the candle out. He'll go ballistic when he sees it.'

But he was too late, and the door swung open to reveal the security guard. He looked at the beer cans and the cards.

'What's going on here?' he demanded.

'Just an innocent game of cards,' said O'Reilly.

Marshall looked at the candle.

'Put that out,' he said. 'You'll start a fire.'

This time, Hendrick did move to extinguish the flame, but a look from Lowther stayed his hand.

'I said put the candle out,' said Marshall.

Lowther stood up and walked over to him.

'You're not going to get funny about this, are you?' he said, a hint of menace in his voice.

'I'll have to report what has happened here,' said Marshall. He moved over to the candle. 'And this is dangerous.'

As he reached out, Lowther grabbed his arm.

'Hey, what the…' exclaimed Marshall. He twisted his arm free and headed for the door. 'I'm going to report the lot of you.'

'Oh, no, you don't,' exclaimed Lowther.

In the struggle that followed, he snapped out a fist and caught Marshall a blow on the cheek. The security guard gave a gasp and *stumbled backwards into the table bearing the candle, which started to rock. Marshall slipped on a patch of grease, catching his head on the edge of a workbench as he crashed to the ground and lay still and silent. As the men watched aghast, no one noticed the candle tip onto its side and flames spring up. By the time they did, it was too late. As he left the room, the last thing Sydney Hendrick saw was the flickering flames dancing across the workshop, reflected in Albert Pembridge's eyes.*

The detectives listened intently, reliving in their own minds the scene in the grimy workshop as the fire rapidly took hold, the flames licking their way voraciously across the workbench.

'There was panic, the place was filling with smoke, and the flames were everywhere,' said Hendrick softly. His face was ashen as he stood once more in the workshop, his lips trembling, the tears glistening in his eyes. 'We all ran out, which was when we realised that James Marshall had not got back up. Patrick rushed back into the room but was beaten back by the flames. He said James was still lying on the floor and we could still get him out... He was all for going back in again, but Bill pulled him back, said we were all for it if he told his story.'

'So, you left him?' breathed Allatt, appalled at what she was hearing.

'We rang 999 once we got out. Anonymously.'

'Nevertheless.'

The old man nodded.

'We left him to die,' he said.

'But he didn't, did he?' said Blizzard. 'He survived, if you can call it surviving. Spent a year in hospital recovering from his burns, then the rest of his days in and out of nursing homes.'

'Yes,' said Hendrick.

'And he never told anyone what happened?' asked Allatt.

'I don't think he really knew,' said Hendrick. 'He took a bang to the head and, when he could speak, he told Dennis Briley that it was all a blur. Besides, he was scared of what Albie and Bill would do to him.'

'And you all told the same story, so it was his word against yours,' said Blizzard. 'One man against five.'

'That's right, yes. The company wanted it all hushed up anyway because they were worried about the bad publicity. They were in financial trouble and contracts would have been cancelled, men would have lost their jobs. They sacked Bill and Harold for bringing the beer in and gave the rest of us reprimands, but that was all that happened. The coroner returned an accidental verdict. Even the police accepted it.'

'Dennis Briley didn't,' said Blizzard.

'I think he was told to forget it,' said Hendrick. 'The deputy chief constable's teenage son had just started at Claytons and he would have been among the first to go if they had made people redundant. Ironic, really; a year or so later, the factory closed anyway and we were all out of work.'

'It would certainly explain why there's no official record of what really happened,' said Blizzard.

'And I imagine that James is dead by now,' said Hendrick sadly. 'Poor man.'

'Actually, he's not. He's in a nursing home in the city, but he's far too sick to talk to us. However, I think that he did eventually remember what happened that night, or at least he summoned up the courage to tell someone. I think that someone is our killer, and he's paying you all back. One by one. And you're the only one left alive. You're next.'

'Oh my God,' croaked the old man. 'What can I do?'

'You'll have to hope that we offer you more protection from the flames than you did for James Marshall,' said Blizzard.

He stood up and the detectives walked into the hallway.

'You're not leaving me?' wailed the old man.

'I have other things to attend to. Besides, he'll not strike in daylight and your house has been the subject of an undercover surveillance operation for the past 24 hours.'

'I haven't seen anyone.'

'It wouldn't be much of an undercover operation if you had.' Blizzard opened the front door. 'We'll be back when it gets dark. Don't try going anywhere. My officers are under orders to arrest you if you so much as poke your nose outside. Good day, Mr Hendrick.'

'Do you know who it is?' asked Hendrick as the officers stepped into the gathering afternoon gloom. 'Do you know who's coming for me?'

Blizzard turned back to face him.

'I do,' he said.

'Who is it?'

'He is your worst nightmare,' said the inspector and headed for his car parked on the lane.

After the vehicle had gone, Hendrick looked along the road, seeking out the undercover officers, but saw no one, so he turned back into the house. Once the front door had closed, the old man sat alone and silent in the deepening darkness of his living room, tears streaming down his cheeks as the memories came crowding in.

Chapter thirty-two

'We getting anywhere with Pete Hooper?' asked Blizzard.

Ramsey and Colley shook their heads.

'Nada,' said Colley.

The three men were sitting with forensics chief Graham Ross in Blizzard's office, eating sandwiches and drinking tea as they grabbed a quick break before the evening's operation. Big Pete Hooper had maintained his sullen silence throughout the interview, except to deny with a guttural grunt the attack on George Ferris. He was now back in his cell.

'Denies even knowing Ferris,' said Ramsey. He took a bite of his sandwich. 'Same with the others. No comment, no comment, no comment. D'Arcy's telling them all that they'll only make things worse if they say anything.'

'He could be right,' said Blizzard. 'You not got anything, Versace?'

'Not enough to support charges, I am afraid,' said Ross. 'And nothing to tie them to the first two fires either. Ferris was the key, and now that he's dead...'

Silence settled on the room for a few moments.

'I can't see that we have any alternative but to let them go,' said Ramsey eventually. 'The CPS agrees. They say that we should bail them.'

'Well, I'm damned if I'm letting them walk,' said Blizzard. He stood up. 'And I want Les Melcham as well.'

'Have a go at them, by all means,' said Ramsey. 'But I'm telling you, guv, we've tried every trick in the book and they're not talking.'

'Ah, yes,' said Blizzard with a slight smile. 'The book.'

'I hate to think what that means,' said Ramsey when the inspector had left the room.

* * *

Ten minutes later, Blizzard and Ramsey were sitting in the interview room, staring across the table at Hooper and his lawyer Paul D'Arcy. Hooper eyed the DCI calmly; John Blizzard may have been respected and feared among the criminal fraternity for his tough questioning, but Hooper knew that, on this occasion, he had the upper hand. His lawyer had told him so.

'I take it you have come to tell my client that he is going to be released,' said D'Arcy.

'Actually, I have come to tell him that he and his pals are being kept in overnight, and that they will be charged with murder first thing in the morning,' said Blizzard. 'I just need to find my Biro.'

Hooper looked stunned, as did D'Arcy. Even Chris Ramsey was struggling to conceal his surprise. Blizzard stood up and made as if to leave the room.

'Hang on,' said D'Arcy. 'You can't do this.'

'Yes, I can. We are holding them while we make further inquiries.' Blizzard shook his head and headed for the door. 'It's a pity really, I don't think for one moment that they meant to kill George Ferris.'

'You don't?'

'No, I think that their instructions were to rough him up to stop him talking about the fires. However, given that none of them are talking, we have no alternative but to pursue murder charges.'

'I very much doubt that the CPS agrees with your assessment, Chief Inspector.'

'That's what you think, Mr D'Arcy. Mind, it does seem rather unfair that Pete and his mates are facing lengthy prison terms when the man who ordered them to do it walks away scot-free. Now, if your client was prepared to be more co-operative…'

'Co-operative how?' D'Arcy's tone was suspicious.

Blizzard sat down again.

'Well,' he said, 'if he confirmed that Les Melcham told them to attack Ferris to cover up for the first fires, the ones in Matthew Street and German Street, I might be able to persuade the CPS to consider manslaughter. Or, maybe, even just assault. As for the fires themselves, well, no one was injured, the damage was only minor; I am sure that we can come up with something. You'll still serve time, as will your mates, Pete, but nowhere near as much.'

'A cheap shot, Chief Inspector,' said D'Arcy. 'You just won't leave Les Melcham alone, will you?'

'Yeah, well, I ain't spragging on Les,' said Hooper.

'Fair enough.'

And without speaking further, Blizzard headed out of the room, followed by Ramsey.

'Jesus, guv,' said Ramsey when they were out in the corridor with the door closed behind them, 'you do sail close to the wind.'

'Sometimes you have to, Chris.'

'Yes, but there's no way that the CPS will back you if you try to charge them with murder with what we've got. You know that.'

'Yes, but Pete Hooper doesn't, does he?'

'No, I guess not,' said Ramsey. 'So, what do we do now?'

'We give him a night in the cells.' Blizzard headed along the corridor. 'It's amazing what four walls can do to a mind at four in the morning. Just ask Andy Hemmings.'

* * *

Shortly before 4pm, Sarah Allatt parked her car outside the detached house on the edge of Brightsea, a small town an hour and a half's drive from Hafton. Sitting next to her, a fellow detective glanced at the piece of paper she was holding, then across at the house.

'This is it,' she said.

The officers got out of the vehicle and opened the gate. By the time they had arrived at the house, the front door had been opened by a man in his late fifties.

'Can I help you?' he asked. His voice was guarded, his expression suspicious.

The detectives held up their warrant cards.

'DS Allatt, Hafton CID.' Allatt gestured to her colleague. 'This is DC Haines. Is this where Emma Marshall lives?'

'Emma Cahill. The name's Cahill.'

'But she was Emma Marshall, yes? Once married to James Marshall?'

The man hesitated.

'Yes,' he said eventually. 'But you're too late. She died three months ago. Cancer. Why do you want to talk to her anyway?'

'We are investigating a series of fatal house fires in Hafton. We thought she might be able to help us. Can we come in, please?'

Still, he continued to block their way.

'I don't want the past dragging up,' he said. 'And I don't want to be involved.'

'It's too late for that, don't you think?' said Allatt. 'You could be charged with obstructing the course of justice.'

He sighed.

'How did you find out?' he asked.

'We found a hospital record from twenty years ago and traced it through to the adoption agency. Look, can we come in? I don't really want to discuss this on the doorstep.' Allatt noticed curtains twitching in a couple of the neighbouring houses. 'And neither, I would suggest, do you.'

Cahill nodded and stood aside to let her through.

'I guess it's time for this to end,' he said.

Chapter thirty-three

Shortly before seven thirty, a large group of expectant officers gathered in the briefing room at Abbey Road to receive their final instructions on the evening's operation, all eying the chief inspector intently as he took his place beside Arthur Ronald at the front.

'Thank you for your attendance, ladies and gentlemen,' said Blizzard. Whispered conversations died away and the room went silent. 'I am afraid that it could turn out to be a long night for you. You will all have had the chance to study the notes in front of you by now and you will be briefed independently, but does anyone have any questions at this stage?'

'Is the target armed?' asked one officer, scanning his piece of paper. 'It doesn't say so here.'

'As far as we can ascertain, no. And the only person in danger appears to be Mr Hendrick. However, we are taking no risks and members of the tactical firearms squad will be involved in tonight's operation. At this stage, I perhaps ought to also explain the presence of one or two faces who may be unfamiliar to you, although, I am sure you all know Johnny Morgan from his Abbey Road days. Sorry to keep you from your tea, old son, this won't take long. Maud in the canteen is delighted to see you back here. Profits have been down since you left.'

A ripple of laughter ran round the room as everyone glanced over to the far corner where a tubby plain-clothed officer in his mid-thirties raised a hand and gave a cheerful grin.

'As most of you will be aware, Johnny is now with the Surveillance Unit,' continued Blizzard. 'In addition to keeping an eye on Sydney Hendrick's cottage, they have also been watching the target. As far as we can ascertain, he has no idea that we are onto him. I cannot stress too much that the key to this operation is total secrecy, so follow your instructions to the letter. We have mainly circumstantial evidence, so we need to catch him in the act. However, one mistake and we might lose our guy forever.'

He let his gaze roam across each and every face.

'So, don't fuck it up,' he said.

By mid-evening, operation Blank Verse – the name suggested with a fine sense of poetic irony by Colley – was well under way. Surveillance officers continued to watch the target's home while plain-clothed colleagues took up their positions in Erinthorpe village, several houses having been taken over with the consent of bemused local residents, other officers hiding in gardens or unmarked vehicles parked out of sight down drives and leafy side roads. Officers in the upstairs bedroom of the house opposite Hendrick's cottage maintained constant surveillance as they had all day. Because the old man's home backed onto an open field ringed by a small wood, others had concealed themselves amid the trees, fortified against the biting cold by thermos flasks. As the teams settled down patiently to wait, they knew that it could be many hours before they saw action.

As the hours dragged by, Hendrick paced about restlessly behind the drawn curtains of the cottage, rubbing his hands anxiously. Blizzard stared moodily into the coal fire and Colley dozed in an armchair, half an ear cocked for any noise which might give away the killer's presence. However, the only sound apart from the crackling fire was the ticking of the grandfather clock. Time passed ponderously and, shortly after eleven thirty, Blizzard switched out the lights, plunging the room into darkness save for the glowing embers in the grate.

And still they waited.

'Are you sure he'll come?' asked Hendrick. He glanced up at the clock from the chair in which he had sat nervously for the past hour and a half.

'He'll come alright,' said Blizzard. 'He's got a job to finish – and this is his time.'

'But who is he? If you know who he is, please tell me. I need to know.'

'You already do,' said Blizzard. The ghost of a smile played on his lips as he said quietly, 'Tell me about Emma.'

'James's wife? Why on earth would you ask about her?'

'Did you know her?'

'Met her once. Nice enough, as I recall, but she walked out on him while he was still in hospital.'

'She must have been through a lot.'

'She had, poor woman. It's hardly surprising that she couldn't cope, really. I mean, I don't think he knew it at the time, but it turned out she was pregnant when James was...' Hendrick's voice tailed off as he gazed at the chief inspector in horror. 'Oh, my God, you don't think...'

'I think that this is all about the baby, yes. And I think that the man we are waiting for is James Marshall's son. The baby whose father never held him, the boy who grew up not even knowing who his real father was.'

Hendrick closed his eyes.

'Are you sure' he asked.

'I am sure, yes,' said Blizzard. 'Emma could not bear the idea that her child would grow up with a father who was so badly disfigured, so she created a new life for herself. Remarried. A chap called Cahill. Trouble was, her new husband did not want the boy, so they had him adopted. The lad found out earlier this year and set out to find his real parents. By the time he had found Emma, she was dying of cancer, but she told him everything before she died. We can only imagine the impact on him. You and your pals robbed the boy of the life he should have had, and now he knows it.'

'No wonder he wants to kill me.'

'No wonder,' said Blizzard. 'In my experience, there are few stronger motives for murder than revenge. It unhinges people.'

The crackle of Colley's radio cut through the silence, making the two men jump and jerking awake the slumbering sergeant.

'Just heard from one of our lot,' said a low voice. They recognised it as Johnny Morgan, who was sitting in a car at the end of the village. 'Looks like chummy's coming out to play, gentlemen. He's got a jerry can with him.'

'Excellent,' said Colley. He rubbed the sleep from his eyes. 'Remember, they should maintain their distance and let him come.'

'Understood,' said Morgan.

'Relax,' said Blizzard, noticing Hendrick's anxious expression. 'There's no way he can get to you. There's more policemen in this village than at the Christmas party.'

'There's probably as much alcohol, mind,' said Colley. I noticed Donny Beresford slipping a hip flask into his pocket as he left Abbey Road.'

The radio soon crackled into life again, providing constant updates on the battered old Ford Escort as it made its way out of Hafton and along the narrow winding country road towards the village. Blizzard and Colley listened with mounting excitement, acutely aware that they were just moments away from arresting the man who had dominated their lives for days.

'Keep coming, you bastard,' murmured the chief inspector. 'Just keep coming.'

'Another couple of minutes and we've got him,' said Colley. He glanced at Hendrick as he sat rigid in his chair. 'Are you alright?'

'Not the word I would have used, Sergeant.'

'The car's in the village,' announced Morgan's voice. 'He's parking at the bottom of Water Lane. Looks like he's going the rest of the way on foot.'

'Let him,' said Blizzard. He glanced at Colley, whose eyes glowed white in the half-light cast by the guttering fire. 'Ready?'

'Ready,' said the sergeant, throat dry, heart thumping, palms sweating.

They strained to hear any sound which would give the killer's movements away and could just make out the faint click of the garden gate, followed by the furtive padding of feet on the path along the side of the cottage.

'He's going round the back,' hissed Blizzard.

'Oh my God,' moaned Hendrick. His face was pale and drawn in the half-light.

Moments later, there was a muffled splintering sound as the back door was forced and swung open with a protesting squeak from its rusty hinge. The footsteps made their way across the kitchen floor and then the living room door creaked open, and they saw the shadowy shape of the intruder illuminated by the embers of the coal fire. The detectives heard the sound of a lid being unscrewed and the sharp smell of petrol.

'Now!' cried Blizzard. He hurled himself across the room.

'What the…!' exclaimed the startled intruder and threw himself backwards into the kitchen, slamming the door in the chief inspector's face.

Blizzard grunted in pain and fell to his knees. Colley barged past the prostrate chief inspector, shoulder-charged the door in best rugby fashion and burst into the kitchen, rolling across the floor before springing to his feet. His quarry twisted around and lashed out with a gloved fist, catching the sergeant full in the face and sending him crashing backwards, screaming out in pain as his head struck the sharp edge of the fridge with a sickening thud. As Colley lay there stunned for a few moments, the intruder wrenched open the back door and escaped into the night.

'All units move in!' yelled Blizzard into his radio as he struggled to his feet in the living room.

Cursing and slapping a handkerchief to his bleeding nose, he gave chase while the shocked Sydney Hendrick slumped in his chair, clasping his chest and fighting for breath, his eyes rolling. Outside in the chill night, the intruder had started to run across the garden when two police officers loomed out of the darkness. With a frightened shout, the suspect lashed out and there was a metallic thud and a muffled exclamation as the petrol can smashed in one policeman's face, sending him crashing sideways into a bush. Ducking under the next blow, Johnny Morgan grabbed the fleeing man but was also sent flying as the arsonist lashed out desperately and wriggled free from the officer's grasp.

Colley hauled himself to his feet in the kitchen, shook his head to clear his vision and staggered outside, blood pouring from a gash behind his left ear. On seeing the other officers sprawling on the ground and hearing the snapping of branches as the suspect crashed through the bushes, he gave chase.

The intruder reached the far end of the garden where there was a small stone wall, which he hurdled with a single leap, throwing the petrol can at the chasing Colley as he did so. The sergeant ducked the missile and scrambled after him. Dimly visible ahead of him, he could see the man running with difficulty through the cloying mud of the field as to his right several officers emerged from nearby woods. His quarry veered away but was no match for Colley. Soon the sergeant was almost upon him and launched himself into a flying rugby tackle which caught the man around the midriff and knocked all the wind out of him. Policeman and suspect crashed to the ground, Colley twisting the killer's arm behind his back and forcing his face deep into the mud. Seconds later, Sarah Allatt emerged from the darkness, running at pace.

'Need a hand?' she asked.

Blowing hard, the sergeant nodded and Allatt reached down to make sure that the man remained on the ground. Colley stayed down on his haunches. Seconds later, other officers were on the scene and took hold of the suspect, allowing Allatt to release her grip. Among them was one of the rugby-playing officers who had assisted with the arrest of Pete Hooper earlier in the day.

'I knew running round a rugby pitch after you would come in handy one day,' said Colley. Still panting heavily from his exertions, he accepted the detective's helping hand as he stood up.

'It's nice to see someone else get the treatment for once,' said the officer. He slapped the sergeant heartily on the shoulder, so hard that Colley winced. 'All that fitness training obviously paid off, which is more than I can say for your guvn'r, I am afraid.'

Unceremoniously, he reached down and hauled the struggling suspect to his feet, whirling him round to face Blizzard, who was battling towards them through the mud, breathing heavily, chest heaving.

'All yours,' said the detective.

'Edward Jones,' gasped Blizzard. He gave himself a moment or two to catch his breath, 'I am arresting you on suspicion of murder…'

Chapter thirty-four

Abbey Road Police Station was buzzing with excitement as the sullen prisoner was locked in the cells and the exultant officers celebrated triumph after their long, cold wait. The aches and pains from chilled bones seemed to melt away as they basked in the warmth of reflected glory, and delighted officers slapped each other on the back as the corridors filled with the excited chatter and the explosive popping of corks from champagne bottles, purchased earlier that day by a now beaming Arthur Ronald in anticipation of success.

In the briefing room, a grinning Colley, glass in hand and a large plaster on his head, revelled in the attention as he was surrounded by an excited throng of colleagues wanting to shake his hand and hear how he made the arrest. For a sergeant more accustomed to the hard, often dispiriting, foot-slogging grind of investigations, it was a moment to relish.

Not that it lasted long because shortly afterwards Blizzard, who had always disliked the party atmosphere of such occasions and whose mood was made bleaker by his aching and swollen nose, summoned him to the interview room where Edward Jones eyed the detectives across the table with a cold detachment, having refused the offer of a lawyer.

'So, when did you find out about your father?' asked Blizzard. 'I assume it was recently?'

'Like you don't know.'

'But I want to hear it from you.'

'This year. I had been looking for my real parents for some time. By the time I discovered where my mother was, it was July and she was dying. She told me where my father was.'

'Did she know the truth behind what happened at the workshop?'

'Suspected, yes; knew, no. She didn't want to talk about it anyway. Said that part of her life was history.'

'So, presumably, it was your father who told you what really happened?'

'He didn't want to at first, but I kept asking.' The replies were being delivered in clipped, clinical tones, devoid of emotion. 'His condition worsened after I told him that Mum was dead, and I think he felt that he had to tell someone before he joined her. It was like a great burden was lifted from him.'

'He could have told us,' said Blizzard. 'We could have arrested them.'

'He thought that unlikely after all these years. Besides, I think he was still frightened of them. Pembridge went to see him several times in the early years. Making sure that he kept quiet.'

'So, how did you find him and the others?' asked Colley.

'It wasn't that difficult. My father knew where most of them were. It was easy enough to get a flat in the same house as Bill Lowther.'

'But why kill them?' asked the sergeant. 'I mean, what a pointless waste of life.'

'And what happened to my father wasn't pointless?' snapped the young man vehemently, his cool veneer breaking as he spat out the words. 'My father suffered twenty years of agony thanks to them. There was no way they weren't going to pay for that.'

* * *

The attendant at the 24-hour petrol station couldn't help thinking it was odd when the man drove onto the forecourt shortly after three o'clock in the morning and filled a can at the pump. Normally, people filling cans had run out of petrol and arrived on foot having abandoned their cars. When the man paid through the grille, the attendant tried to see his face, but it was cast in shadow by the hood of his anorak and he couldn't make out any of the features. Then the man melted into the night. The attendant shrugged, thought nothing more of it and returned to his crossword puzzle.

* * *

'But why kill them so horribly?' asked Blizzard in the oppressive atmosphere of the interview room.

'They had to feel what my father felt,' said Jones.

'But you killed them in their sleep,' said Colley.

'You really don't think I let them die in ignorance, do you?' Jones smiled. 'No, I made sure they were awake. Even though Pembridge was out of it, he knew that his worst nightmares had come true. I could see it in his eyes. No point in doing it otherwise, was there?'

'Jesus,' murmured Colley, sitting back in his chair. 'You're sick.'

'And what about what they did to my father? His body underwent so many skin grafts that it looks like patchwork. He's spent twenty years in and out of hospitals and nursing homes. If you want to talk about sick, Sergeant, talk about the bastards who left him to burn to death.'

'But killing them just perpetuates the evil,' said Colley.

'Well, they do say evil begets evil.' Jones laughed bitterly. 'I never really knew my father. Do you know what that means? All I have to cling to is the image of a horribly scarred man old before his time, dying in a nursing home reeking of antiseptic and stale urine. What kind of memory is that?'

Despite his horror at the murders, Colley found himself nodding. It was a purely instinctive reaction. Even though they knew that Marshall could not speak to them, he and Blizzard had gone to see him the previous day and the memory was still vivid in the sergeant's mind. The former security guard had been lying in a darkened room at the nursing home, hands trembling uncontrollably, skin deathly pale, eyes lifeless, as he waited for release from his years of suffering. James Marshall had gone through more than any man should have to bear, and the experience of seeing him had disturbed both the sergeant and his chief inspector, so much so that neither had spoken of it since. Neither were convinced that they could summon up the words.

'And he wasn't the only victim,' continued Jones, breaking the silence that had settled on the stuffy little room. 'They destroyed my mother as well.'

'Tell me about her,' said Blizzard. He shifted in his chair as his bad back gave a twinge.

'She suffered as well,' said Jones bitterly. Emotion had replaced the coldness of the early stages of the interview. 'I don't blame her for walking out on him after what she went through, but she blamed herself. Spent the rest of her life tormenting herself for what she did. Too ashamed to go back and see my father, and too ashamed to come looking for me. So, you see, you may view me as a murderer but I'm a victim as well. I lost everything. They might as well have left *me* for dead that night.'

'But was it worth killing them?' asked Blizzard. Back still twinging, he walked over to lean against the wall, hands thrust deep into his pockets.

'Oh yes,' breathed Jones softly. He looked up at him with a glint in his eyes. 'I'm glad they burned.'

A shiver ran down the chief inspector's spine. It was a sensation he had felt before, when looking into the eyes of Reginald Morris.

* * *

The drunken man lurching home along the main road through the western outskirts of Hafton shortly after three fifteen that morning, thought little of the car which drove slowly past him in the direction of Erinthorpe village. Staggering onto the grass verge to avoid the vehicle, the drunk leant unsteadily against a lamppost and tried to make out the features of its driver. But it was dark and his eyes weren't focusing properly, so he couldn't distinguish anything. Thinking nothing more of it, he weaved his way back onto the road and kept going, promising himself as he shuffled along that he would never drink this much again. Just like he always did.

* * *

'So, does your father know what you have done?' asked Blizzard. He returned to sit next to Colley.

'No,' said Jones. 'He would have asked me not to go through with it. That's the kind of man he is, and I couldn't risk him telling someone. I was going to tell him when they were all dead. Not sure he'd have understood, though. I don't think he knows anything anymore, do you?'

Blizzard thought back to the visit to the nursing home.

'I suspect you're right,' he said. 'Tell me about The Cedars. I can understand O'Reilly but why kill the other residents?'

'That is the only thing I regret. Honest to God, I didn't mean to kill them all, but the place just went up so quickly, it was unbelievable.'

'Not that it will help you,' said Colley, 'but The Cedars broke just about every fire safety rule in the book and the owner has been told that she will be prosecuted.'

'Good. There's as much blood on her hands.'

'That's a question of interpretation,' replied the sergeant.

'Well, I hope she goes to jail anyway,' Jones said.

'Well, that's something I think we can both agree on,' said Blizzard. 'There's one other thing I need to clear up. Presumably, you set out to frame Andy Hemmings?'

'It was a shitty trick, but there was no alternative.'

'But why drag Reginald Morris into it?'

'He was a smokescreen,' said Jones. He chuckled drily. 'So to speak. I remembered Andy telling me how he visited Morris in Crake Lane with that Marriott fellow. Andy told me how Morris used to send poetry to the police, and the rest was easy. Easy enough to fake Andy's handwriting. Close enough to get you thinking anyway. And it worked, didn't it? Confused the hell out of you.'

'It certainly did,' said Blizzard thoughtfully. 'In fact, there's a certain artistic elegance to it that's almost too good for a humble electrician, Edward. It's too clever by half.'

The chief inspector was convinced that he detected a hint of concern flit across the young man's face. But it was just a hint, and it had gone as soon as it appeared.

* * *

The poacher, loping across the icy furrows of the moonlit field with trusty hound at heel shortly after three thirty that clear, cold autumn morning, thought it odd when he saw the car driving slowly along the country lane towards Erinthorpe with its headlights extinguished. Warily, he dropped to his haunches and beckoned the dog to sit silently by his side. Poaching banished from his mind, he crouched behind a threadbare hedge and watched intently, as the vehicle reversed through a gateway on the far side of the field so that it was hidden from anyone passing along the road and cut its engine.

In the silence that followed, the poacher heard the faint click of a door opening and watched intrigued as the hooded driver got out and started to walk along the country lane in the direction of the village a mile away, carrying something bulky in his hand. Hard as he peered, the poacher could not make out what it was, although it looked like some form of container.

The poacher gave a sigh of resignation; there had been enough activity in the area that night and even though all the police had gone now, the last thing he needed was a stranger wandering about. Reluctantly, he decided to call it a night and with a low whistle he summoned his dog, shouldered his sack, and headed across the field towards the city and home, cheered by thoughts of a hot toddy and the enveloping warmth of his bed.

Behind him, the stranger continued to walk at a steady pace in the opposite direction along the road. For him, the night was not over yet. For him, there was work to do.

* * *

'But surely,' said Blizzard as he paced slowly around the room trying to keep calm, his unease growing rapidly now, 'you knew we would see through your little charade soon enough?'

'I imagined you would,' said Jones. 'I hope you've released Andy. He's been through enough on my account as it is.'

'We let him leave three hours ago,' said Colley.

'I'm glad.'

'We'd suspected for a while that it wasn't him,' said Blizzard.

'It didn't really matter if you worked it out. All I needed was to buy myself a little time. I was going to give myself up after I killed the last one anyway. Do the old insanity act.'

'But you haven't killed the last one, have you?' said Blizzard. 'You've failed, haven't you? I mean Sydney Hendrick is alive, isn't he?'

'Is he?' asked Jones and smiled. He looked at the wall clock. Three forty-five. 'Is he really?'

He sat back and folded his arms.

'Well,' he said, 'I think we've talked long enough, don't you, gentlemen?'

A chill ran down the chief inspector's spine and tingled the hairs on the back of his neck. With a jolt, he realised that he had felt the icy sensation before, felt it when Reginald Morris entered his mind during unguarded moments at dead of night, felt it when his detective's instincts screamed out that something was wrong, horribly wrong. That he had missed something. That the puzzle was incomplete.

Images of a blazing cottage flashed into the chief inspector's mind, images of a man grotesquely silhouetted in the eerie orange glow of a window engulfed by flames, clawing at the glass in his desperation to get out.

'Oh, my God,' breathed the chief inspector. He clapped a hand to his mouth in horror.

'What's wrong?' said Colley.

'Now, he understands,' said Jones softly. His features hardened. 'And he will consume alive those who slept at dead of night. And you're too late, Chief Inspector.'

'I've been such a fool,' groaned Blizzard. He leapt to his feet and jabbed a finger at Edward Jones. 'I thought all this Reginald Morris nonsense was too clever for you! The bastard's got an accomplice! And I know who it is.'

* * *

The hooded man entered the village.

Chapter thirty-five

Blizzard edged his car through the cordon of patrol vehicles that had just arrived to seal off Water Lane in Erinthorpe again and pulled up outside the cottage. He knew that Sydney Hendrick was still at home because, when a doctor had recommended that the shocked pensioner be taken to hospital for a check-up, he had refused, insisting that there was nothing wrong with him. With Edward Jones under arrest, Blizzard had seen no reason to argue with a truculent old man and the police had packed up and melted into the night, leaving Erinthorpe to its darkness.

Now, they were back in force and Blizzard stood in the stillness, surveying the cottage pensively. Behind him, a crowd of excited villagers had gathered in their nightclothes as rows of flashing blue lights illuminated the night sky once more, and police officers quickly fanned out along the streets, a number of them carrying guns. Behind the cottage, a team of armed officers picked their way carefully across the fields whilst the faint clatter of rotor blades overhead signalled the approach of the police helicopter. The distant guttural throb of engines heralded the imminent arrival of Blue Watch as the chief inspector unclipped the front gate and walked tentatively up the path, followed closely by Colley.

'It all looks pretty peaceful to me,' whispered the sergeant. 'Are you sure about this? Could just be Eddie Jones playing more games. What if you're wrong?'

'I think our Sydney will be well naffed off if we wake him up from the first untroubled sleep he's had in twenty years.'

'Less of the we. This is your idea.'

'Thanks a bunch,' said Blizzard. He hammered loudly on the front door. From the inside of the cottage, came a loud crash followed by a whooshing sound, startled cries and the unmistakable sound of flames taking hold.

'Look!' cried Colley in horror.

He pointed to the ground floor bedroom curtains which had been thrown open to reveal a raging inferno within. Silhouetted by the dancing orange flames was Sydney Hendrick, his face twisted in agony, his mouth gaping in a silent scream, his spindly hands clawing frantically at the glass. For a few moments, Blizzard stood rigid, rooted to the spot by the nightmarish vision of the old man's scrabbling hands disappearing from view as he was swallowed up by billowing smoke.

Colley was the first to react, shoulder-charging the front door and tumbling into the hallway, which was starting to fill with smoke. As the sergeant sprawled on the floor, Blizzard regained his senses and ran in after him, catching a glimpse as he leapt over the threshold of a shadowy shape darting into the living room. With a cry he gave chase, sprinting into the kitchen, but the intruder was too quick and wrenched open the back door to dive out into the night. Blizzard made to follow but was called back by a frantic yell from his sergeant.

'Leave him!' cried Colley, struggling to his feet and blundering through the smoke. 'We've got to get Hendrick out!'

Blizzard hesitated, torn between the fleeing arsonist and his duty to save life. Colley shared no such dilemma and kicked open the bedroom door, sending flames and smoke billowing out into the hallway. Hurling himself to the floor and clasping a handkerchief to his mouth, the sergeant disappeared into the room. With a curse, Blizzard took one last glance at the fleeing intruder and followed his sergeant.

Through the dancing flames and the black, choking smoke, the detectives could see that the curtains and the bed were alight and that Sydney Hendrick had collapsed in the corner of the room, his legs twisted beneath him and his skin starting to peel and blister. Instinctively and despite the heat scorching their own faces, the officers grabbed the unconscious old man and half-carried, half-dragged him out of the cottage where they sank to their knees, coughing and gratefully breathing in gulps of welcome fresh air.

'That was too close for comfort,' gasped Colley. His eyes glowed white out of a blackened face as green-jacketed paramedics rushed forward. 'Are you all right?'

'I've been better,' croaked Blizzard feebly. He rolled over and retched, then pointed weakly at the lifeless form of Sydney Hendrick lying on the grass. 'What about him?'

'Not brilliant,' replied a paramedic. She dropped to her knees and listened to the old man's shallow, rattling breathing. 'Not good at all.'

'Where's the bastard that did this?' asked Colley. He started to get to his feet, then doubled up as he was seized by a violent coughing fit.

'He got out the back,' replied Blizzard. He looked up hopefully as a uniformed inspector ran towards them. 'Well – did you get him?'

'I'm afraid not. We couldn't get our lads into place quickly enough and he gave them the slip across the fields. But the chopper should find him. He won't escape, sir.'

'I'm not worried if he does,' said Blizzard. He took another deep breath of air and accepted a helping hand from the inspector as he stood up.

'You're not?' asked the surprised officer. He had been expecting a furious reaction from the chief inspector, even in his debilitated state.

'It's finished,' said Blizzard. He gestured at the firefighters battling their way into the burning cottage. 'There's only one place for him to run to now.'

He turned and caught sight of a familiar face.

'Are you all right?' asked Tom Spivey. 'A few seconds later you and your Mr Hendrick would have been a goner.'

'He might still be.' Blizzard nodded at the ambulance crew carrying the recumbent pensioner down the path on a stretcher.

'At least he's got a chance,' replied Spivey. He looked at Colley. 'You've both shown remarkable courage.'

'Thank you,' said Blizzard sincerely, recalling the strained conversation the last time they met outside Harold Bainbridge's gutted bungalow. 'We owe you at least that.'

'But do me a favour,' said Spivey with a crooked smile. 'I'm actually beginning to dream nostalgically of fighting grass fires – promise me this is the end of it.'

'It's the end of it,' said Blizzard wearily.

Behind them, the roof of the blazing cottage caved in and a cascade of orange sparks leapt into the air.

Chapter thirty-six

The early morning mist was still shrouding The Beeches nursing home – a rambling ivy-covered Victorian house in a leafy western suburb of the city – as the car crunched up the gravel drive. A motionless figure stood outside the building, watching two ambulance officers load a body into the back of their vehicle. He brushed a tear from his cheek as they silently closed the rear doors. Without showing any surprise or alarm, the man looked round, face still obscured by the hood of his anorak, and caught sight of Blizzard and Colley as they got out of the car after waiting to let the ambulance bearing the body of James Marshall pass by.

'Time to go, Andy,' said Blizzard. He gasped as the figure lowered the hood to reveal his face. 'You!'

'I wondered when you'd come,' said the man. He glanced after the departing ambulance. 'He's at peace now.'

'Raymond Marriott,' said Blizzard. He recovered his composure and produced a set of handcuffs. 'I am arresting you on suspicion of murder.'

'They won't be needed,' said the writer. 'I heard it on the radio news – Sydney Hendrick is dead, isn't he?'

'Yes, he suffered a heart attack just after they got him to hospital.'

'He was the last of them. It's over now.'

'But why you?' asked Blizzard. 'Why should you want them dead?'

'Because I am James Marshall's brother.'

'His brother?'

'Yes. I left home when I was a teenager and didn't go back. I never got on with our father and the longer I was away, the more difficult it was to think about returning. I don't think James was that bothered when I left. He never approved of my drug taking.'

'So why come looking for him now?' asked Colley.

'Time moves on. Two years ago, I decided I wanted to see him again. Come back from Holland. Patch things up between us, start anew. So, I began looking for him. You shouldn't take these things to your grave.'

'And you found him here?' said Blizzard. He gestured to the faded grandeur of The Beeches.

'Yes, but it was too late, he hardly knew me. Then I bumped into Eddie on one of the visits. It was him who told me the truth about the fire at Claytons. He told me what he was planning to do.'

'But why go along with it?' Blizzard shook his head in bemusement. 'Why not come to us, for God's sake?'

'Would you have done anything about it, even if we had? Besides, I was angry at being cheated of my brother. Just like my nephew was angry. He was going to do the killing. When he mentioned that he lived in the same house as Andy Hemmings, I remembered that he had been to Crake Lane and suggested we frame him.'

'But you must have realised that your poem would lead us to you as well?'

'What if it did? I knew you wouldn't really think I had anything to do with the fire.' Marriott gave a slight smile. 'After all, poets don't do that sort of thing, do they?'

'How did you know to attack Hendrick's house last night?' asked Colley.

'Edward said that if he didn't call, I should assume he'd been arrested and that I should finish the job myself.' Marriott watched calmly as a patrol car edged its way up the drive and two uniformed officers got out and walked toward him. 'Someone had to.'

'Take him away,' said Blizzard wearily to the officers.

'One thing before I go,' said Marriott. He flashed a smile at the inspector. 'You will mention my new book at the trial, won't you? This kind of thing could do wonders for sales!'

'Suddenly,' said Blizzard as he watched the uniformed officers usher Marriott to the patrol car, 'I feel very tired.'

'Perhaps you should take that holiday which the Super keeps going on about,' said Colley. 'Take Fee and the little 'un.'

'Maybe I should,' said Blizzard. He brushed a hand across his eyes. 'And maybe I won't come back.'

'You'll come back.'

'Aye, you're probably right.'

Digging his hands deep into his pockets, John Blizzard walked down the driveway and disappeared into the mist.

* * *

Several hours later, Blizzard was in his office, finishing off his paperwork and preparing to go home to Fee and the baby for a few snatched hours, when Chris Ramsey walked into the room. Normally a downbeat, humourless individual, the detective inspector was beaming despite his own fatigue.

'What you so pleased about?' asked Blizzard.

'Because I love Christmas.'

'Christmas isn't for seven weeks.'

'Well, you can start celebrating early, if you like. You were right about a night in the cells working wonders on the human mind. Pete Hooper has had second thoughts and given us chapter and verse on Les Melcham.'

Blizzard stared at him in disbelief.

'You're kidding,' he said.

'I've just taken his statement. Turns out that he used his phone call to ring Les Melcham but was told that he was on his own and that he'd better not say anything to us. Put the phone down on our Pete. He's spitting bullets. Says he's not going to take the rap on his own.'

'Nothing more powerful than a villain scorned.'

'Indeed so. Anyway, in return for us putting in a word with the CPS, Pete signed a statement saying that Melcham ordered him and his cronies to start the first two fires, and that he also ordered them to attack George Ferris to cover them up. We've got the bastard, guv.'

'So, it would seem. Good work, Chris, good work indeed.' Blizzard stood up, slapped him on the shoulder and unhooked his coat from the back of the chair. 'Come on. It's time to nick Les Melcham, I think. Jesus, do you know how long I've been waiting to say that?'

'Too long.'

'Too long indeed.'

* * *

They found Melcham standing outside the fire-hit house in Inkerman Street, deep in conversation with a man in a sharp suit. Occasionally, Melcham would gesticulate towards the property, then angrily jab a finger at the man, who looked increasingly uncomfortable under the tirade of furious words.

'Who's he?' asked Blizzard as he parked the car.

'Ironically enough, it's the insurance assessor,' said Ramsey.

Blizzard gave a slight smile and the detectives got out of the car and walked over to the men.

'What do you want?' asked Melcham.

'Just a little chat,' said Blizzard.

'Well, I don't want to talk to you, so fuck off.' Melcham glared as Blizzard stayed where he was. 'Look, if you don't get out of my face, I'll get my lawyer onto you. You can't keep harassing me like this.'

'Can't I now?'

'Na. I'll have you kicked off the force.'

'I'd like to see you try.'

Melcham looked at him uncertainly. Behind the bluster, the officers detected a nervousness at Blizzard's calm demeanour. Melcham turned to the insurance man.

'We'll finish this later,' he said.

'Yeah,' said Blizzard. 'In about twenty years, I should think.'

Melcham stared at him.

'What do you mean by that?' he said.

'Les Melcham,' said Blizzard, 'I am arresting you on suspicion of conspiracy to commit murder and arson with intent to endanger life...'

Melcham stared at him in amazement, then turned and took several paces down the street.

'Oh, go on, add resisting arrest to the list,' said Blizzard. He watched as Melcham turned back, a resigned look on his face. The inspector gave him an affable smile. 'Happy Christmas, Les.'

Blizzard nodded at Ramsey and watched as he placed the handcuffs round the landlord's wrists.

Chapter thirty-seven

It was early one sunny Saturday afternoon in early summer and John Blizzard, dressed in grimy orange overalls and with oil streaking his face, was in the railway shed. He crouched down beside the engine, lovingly scraping rust off the locomotive's boiler. So intent was he on his work that, at first, he did not hear the grinding sound as the shed door was hauled open and David Colley appeared, a sports bag slung over his shoulder. After a few moments, the inspector realised that he was there, and watched as the sergeant picked his way with some difficulty through the piles of scrap metal and antiquated nuts and bolts.

'Now then,' said the sergeant.

'This had better be good,' said Blizzard. 'I promised Fee I'd be back for three and I'm already way behind on what I meant to do. I had all on to persuade her to let me go in the first place. She's had Mikey most of the week.'

'Yeah, I know the feeling,' said Colley gloomily. 'Jay's getting funny about me playing so much rugby.'

'I thought Arthur was going to ban you from playing anyway. Didn't you black Powlett's eye again on Tuesday night?'

'An accident,' smirked Colley.

'I do hope it wasn't. The man's had it coming. Do you know what he did last week? Do you?' Blizzard shook his head. 'I mean, can you believe that he only went and reported me for parking in the wrong place in the yard?'

'Really?' said Colley. 'I'd forgotten that. I mean, it's not like you've mentioned it five hundred times.'

Blizzard gave him a rueful look.

'I guess I have banged on about it,' he said. The inspector homed in on a piece of rust on the boiler and gave it a rub. 'Anyway, what brings you down here on a lovely Saturday afternoon? I thought you were on a half day. Don't tell me that you've suddenly been seized with a passion for steam engines?'

'Er, not quite,' said Colley as he looked round at the tangle of wires and old metal tubing. His face was suddenly serious as he unzipped his bag and produced a familiar brown envelope. 'It's one of these, I'm afraid. Arrived as I was leaving the office.'

He handed it to the inspector. Blizzard turned it over in his hands several times before slowly opening it and withdrawing a single sheet of paper covered in a familiar scrawl. Colley watched as the chief inspector read it slowly, silently mouthing the words and hearing in his mind Reginald Morris's nasal voice as he did so.

'Dear Chief Inspector,' it read, 'I thought you would like to know that I have decided to abandon my efforts to be released from this place. I have grown used to the company of madmen and, after all these years, find it infinitely preferable to life on the outside. Indeed, I have come to believe that the real madmen live in your world and not mine. May I take this opportunity to wish you, Fee and the baby well for your future. Here's hoping, and I am sure that you will take this the right way, that we never meet again. Yours, Reginald Morris.'

'Well?' asked Colley. He eyed the chief inspector with anxious eyes. 'What does it say?'

'Oh, nothing much,' murmured Blizzard. He slipped the sheet of paper back into the envelope. 'Just someone saying goodbye.'

But he knew that, finally, his nightmares had gone, banished by the very man who had caused them in the first place. The only man on earth who had possessed the power to drive them away. In a way, thought the inspector as he handed the envelope back to the sergeant, Reginald Morris had won. His had always been the power, right from that first flicker in the night.

Blizzard patted the locomotive affectionately and looked at the sergeant.

'Come on, let's go.' Blizzard looked at the sergeant's sports bag. 'Do I take it that you are on your way to play rugby?'

'No, just forgot to take it home last night.'

'Jay and Laura still away?'

'Back tomorrow.'

'In which case, then, I'll buy you a pint,' said Blizzard. 'There's a nice little place round the corner. Proper old railmen's boozer. All spit and sawdust.'

'Sounds lovely.'

'You'll like it. Promise.'

'Right.'

The sergeant watched as his boss struggled out of his overalls and hung them on a hook.

'What will you tell Fee?' asked Colley as they headed for the door.

'I'll say that I lost track of time.'

'Yeah, that's the one I try on Jay when she wants me to take Laura to Soft Play.'

'And does it work?' asked Blizzard as he followed the sergeant out into the bright summer sunshine.

'Na.'

Blizzard gave a low laugh, pulled closed the door and snapped on the padlock.

'Let's give it a go anyway,' he said.

Colley grinned at him.

'Why not?' he said.

'Yeah,' said Blizzard. 'Why not indeed?'

THE END

List of characters

Ronnie Burnett – criminal
Paul D'Arcy – lawyer
Arnold Dawlish – lawyer
George Ferris – insurance salesman
Rachel Ferris – George's wife
Sydney Hendrick – villager
Martin Hayley – mental hospital administrator
Mrs Havers – neighbour of Harold Bainbridge
Andrew Hemmings – university student
Pete Hooper – criminal
Edward Jones – electrician
Rosemary Ledwith – niece of Patrick O'Reilly
Bill Lowther – retired shipyard worker
Emma Marshall – former wife of James Marshall
James Marshall – security guard
Raymond Marriott – poet
Maureen – Rachel Ferris's sister
Elaine Harrison – fire brigade investigator
Gary Mistry – journalist
Hazel Myers – mental hospital employee
Patrick O'Reilly – nursing home resident
Graham Parris – criminal
Albert Pembridge – alcoholic pensioner
Glenda Pressley – neighbour of Albert Pembridge
Peter Reynolds – Home Office Pathologist
Tom Spivey – fire brigade Watch Commander
Leonard Wright – university professor

If you enjoyed this book, please let others know by leaving a quick review on Amazon. Also, if you spot anything untoward in the paperback, get in touch. We strive for the best quality and appreciate reader feedback.

editor@thebookfolks.com

www.thebookfolks.com

ALSO BY JOHN DEAN

In this series:

The Long Dead (Book 1)
Strange Little Girl (Book 2)
The Railway Man (Book 3)
The Secrets Man (Book 4)
A Breach of Trust (Book 5)
Death List (Book 6)
The Latch Man (Book 8)
No Age to Die (Book 9)
The Vengeance Man (Book 10)
The Name on the Bullet (Book 11)

In the DCI Jack Harris series:

Dead Hill
The Vixen's Scream
To Die Alone
To Honour the Dead
Thou Shalt Kill
Error of Judgement
The Killing Line
Kill Shot
Last Man Alive
The Girl in the Meadow

Writing as John Stanley:

The Numbers Game
Sentinel

When a routine archaeological dig turns up bodies on the site of a WWII prisoner of war camp, it should be an open and shut case for detective John Blizzard. But forensics discover one of the deaths is more recent and the force have a murder investigation on their hands.

When a family is brutally murdered, one child is never found. It still troubles DCI John Blizzard to this day. But new clues emerge that will take him deep into the criminal underworld and into conflict with the powers that be. Cracking the case will take all of the detective's skills, and more. Coming out unscarred will be impossible.

Veteran crime-solver DCI John Blizzard is confronted
with his hardest case yet when a boxer and wide boy is
found dead in a railway signal box. Someone is determined
to ruin the investigation and prepared to draw the
residents of a local housing estate into a war with the
police to get their way. Has the detective finally met his
match?

While detective John Blizzard looks into a series of drug-
related deaths, his nemesis, gangland thug Morrie Raynor,
is released from prison. Blizzard becomes convinced
Raynor is linked to a new crime spree, but with little
evidence other than the ravings of a sick, delirious man,
the detective's colleagues suspect his personal feelings are
clouding his judgement.

A corrupt industrialist is found dead in his home. When his family shed crocodile tears, DCI John Blizzard turns the screw. But when their alibis check out, can his team track down the real killer among a long list of likely suspects?

An undercover detective is shot in his home. Later, police officers on a routine patrol are fired at. Someone has a big problem with law enforcement. DCI Blizzard starts a crackdown on his city's most notorious gangsters. But is he in danger of rubbing the wrong people up the wrong way? Or is he already on the killer's list?

When a dangerous convicted felon is released from prison, a local church takes the man in. DCI Blizzard has to deal with the community uproar and when a local youth is killed it will take all of the detective's skills to right a wrong.

When a dangerous convicted felon is released from prison, DCI Blizzard makes it clear he is unwelcome on his patch. But when a local church takes the man in, Blizzard has to deal with the community uproar. When a local youth is killed it will take all of the detective's skills to right a wrong.

When a youth is scared out of his wits by a man dressed all in black in the local church graveyard, the police don't think much of his tales about a bogeyman. But when a murder later takes place there, DCI John Blizzard will have to suspend disbelief and work out the identity of The Vengeance Man before he wreaks havoc in the neighbourhood.

When a cop taking part in a reality TV show is shot dead, it makes the police look pretty bad. DCI John Blizzard, no media darling himself, sets to finding the killer. This leads him to lock horns with a renowned gangster who acts like he is above the law. Yet as Blizzard tries to balance the scales of justice, he is thrown a curve ball.

Visit www.thebookfolks.com for more great titles like these!

Made in United States
Orlando, FL
29 March 2024

45132799R00136